"I think we're being followed."

Fran swallowed. "What do we do?"

Tanner thought for a moment. "If I slow down, maybe you can get out and I'll lead him away..."

"I doubt that would work. How would I travel with him?" She jerked her head to indicate the child. "He probably won't react well. We'll have to make it to the police station."

"We might not have a choice," he ground out.

The treacherous road curved around again. He didn't like going so fast when he had passengers without safety seats. "Slide onto the floorboard."

Fran took the child and slid down to the ground. He said a prayer that the child would remain sleeping. If he didn't and tried to fight, not only would it distract Tanner, but it would leave the child more vulnerable.

A bullet crashed through the back window.

The driver behind them was out for blood. Who was the target? If he didn't find a way out, they'd all become the next victims.

Dana R. Lynn grew up in Illinois. She met her husband at a wedding and told her parents she'd met the man she was going to marry. Nineteen months later, they were married. Today, they live in rural Pennsylvania with their three children and a variety of animals. In addition to writing, she works as a teacher for the deaf and hard of hearing, and is active in her church.

Books by Dana R. Lynn

Love Inspired Suspense

Amish Country Justice

Plain Target
Plain Retribution
Amish Christmas Abduction
Amish Country Ambush
Amish Christmas Emergency
Guarding the Amish Midwife
Hidden in Amish Country
Plain Refuge
Deadly Amish Reunion
Amish Country Threats
Covert Amish Investigation
Amish Christmas Escape
Amish Cradle Conspiracy
Her Secret Amish Past
Crime Scene Witness
Hidden Amish Target
Hunted at Christmas
Amish Witness to Murder
Protecting the Amish Child

Visit the Author Profile page at LoveInspired.com for more titles.

Protecting the Amish Child

DANA R. LYNN

LOVE INSPIRED SUSPENSE
INSPIRATIONAL ROMANCE

LOVE INSPIRED SUSPENSE
INSPIRATIONAL ROMANCE

ISBN-13: 978-1-335-98009-0

Recycling programs
for this product may
not exist in your area.

Protecting the Amish Child

Copyright © 2024 by Dana Roae

Love Inspired
22 Adelaide St. West, 41st Floor
Toronto, Ontario M5H 4E3, Canada
www.LoveInspired.com

Printed in U.S.A.

There is no fear in love; but perfect love casteth out fear: because fear hath torment. He that feareth is not made perfect in love.
—*1 John* 4:18

To my daughter Rachael and my son-in-law Joshua, married 9/23/23. I pray your marriage will be richly blessed with faith and love.

ONE

Francesca Brown slipped her feet into her favorite slip-on sandals, the ones with rhinestones along the strap that went across her toes, and took her mug filled with salted caramel tea out to the wraparound porch her grandfather had built fifty years ago. Taking a sip of the steaming tea, she frowned. The air was a bit cool for the end of August, probably due to the near constant precipitation and cloud cover they'd had for the past four days. The rain showed no signs of letting up. She had errands to run in town. While she relished observing a good storm from the safety of her porch and enjoyed listening to the drops land on the roof above her, driving in it was a different matter altogether.

At least the thunderstorms that had pounded on Sutter Springs had dissipated. Sutter Springs was a small town on the outskirts of Berlin County, just a stone's throw from Columbus, Ohio. It was a large tourism attraction for those who wanted to learn about the Amish culture. In Sutter Springs, the Amish and non-Amish lived and worked side by side. When she'd first moved here after she'd married, she'd fallen in love with the town. Since she'd been widowed, she had considered leaving the house she'd shared with her late husband and possibly moving elsewhere.

She couldn't do it, though. This was her home. The one place she felt completely free to be herself.

Sighing, she lifted her mug for another drink. The tea halted halfway to her lips. Fran blinked then narrowed her eyes to bring the perimeter of her lawn into focus, desperate to deny what her mind insisted it saw. Her breath hitched in her throat. A pair of dark shoes, toes pointed toward the sky. From across the yard, it was difficult to make out any details of the footwear. Letting her eyes sweep past the shoes, she tried to get a glimpse of the body attached to them, but visibility was poor in the current weather conditions. She'd have to take a closer look. Setting her mug on the railing, she peered around. When she didn't see anyone else, she took a deep breath and carefully trod down the five steps and onto the sodden grass. The wet blades tickled her sandal-clad feet. Within seconds, her trendy, short fluffy black curls were plastered to her skull and her jeans and cotton sweater were soaked. She ignored the sensation.

Some things were more important than comfort.

Plodding across the lawn, she brushed a hand across her forehead to move the hair out of her eyes and approached the body. She reached behind and plucked her cell phone out of her back pocket. Whether or not she needed an ambulance or the coroner, she needed to call in the situation and request assistance.

Dialing 9-1-1, she held the phone to her ear and continued to stride closer.

"Nine-one-one. What is your emergency?" A soothing voice, just a touch too perky, answered the call.

She let out the breath she'd been holding. Good. Someone she knew. The familiar voice crackled down the line. The signal was horrible in the downpour.

"Leslie, this is Francesca Brown. I have a body in my front yard. I'm not sure if he's dead or alive yet."

"Is the scene safe, Fran?" the dispatcher asked, concern thickening her voice.

"Yes. I don't see anyone else around."

By this time, she'd reached the man on her lawn. He wasn't much more than a kid, his dark eyes staring blankly up at the sky, untroubled by the rain pelting him. She didn't need to touch him to know he was dead, but she squatted beside him and pressed her fingers to the pulse point on his cold neck.

"He's dead."

"You know the drill. Stay on the line. I'm notifying both the police and the coroner."

Fran agreed, resigning herself to remaining outside in the cold rain until someone arrived. She sighed. Fran was a forensic artist contracted with half a dozen police departments in the surrounding area outside Berlin, Ohio, including the Sutter Springs Police Department. She had seen dead people more times than she could recall. It wasn't unusual for her to be asked to reconstruct an image from a skull, and while most people might find it gruesome, Fran had become mostly immune to the macabre aspects of her job. She focused on helping her law enforcement colleagues bring closure to families and justice to criminals. It brought its own kind of satisfaction.

She had no trouble dealing with dead people at work. When a dead body showed up on her front lawn, however, that was a different story.

Glancing again at the face, she frowned, his image nagging at her memory. She had seen his face before. But where? Skimming his features, she paused at the distinct jagged scar on the left side of his jaw. Suddenly, she knew the identity of the deceased young man and exhaled sharply as if she'd been struck in the stomach.

"Leslie, I am nearly certain the dead body is a missing person named Jared Murray."

"The son of the federal judge George Murray? The kid who disappeared several years ago?"

"That's the one. He vanished almost six years ago." She'd never forget. It had been her first case after her husband, Sean, had died following a hit-and-run accident. At her chief's direction, she had gone to the hospital to do a composite of the attackers, and presumed kidnappers, with the judge who'd been attacked in his vehicle when his car got a flat tire on his way to a political event. According to the judge, his seventeen-year-old son had been with him. The judge had been left for dead. An anonymous 9-1-1 call had been received from the judge's phone, but when the police and ambulance arrived on the scene, the phone was lying on the ground and the judge was out cold. Jared was gone. He'd never returned home and none of his neighbors or friends had seen him since he'd left the house with his father earlier that morning. The assumption was that he'd been kidnapped. When no ransom demand was made, everyone feared the worse.

Including Fran.

It was the first time she'd been inside the hospital since her husband's death.

Sean had come into her life when they'd sat next to each other in a forensics class during her sophomore year at college. He'd loved numbers and logic and was a true crime junkie. It hadn't taken him long to decide to channel those interests and become a forensic accountant. She'd never forget his grin the day the FBI had hired him.

He'd been very dedicated to his work. She'd been so

proud of him, right up until the day she'd got the call that he'd been rushed by ambulance to the hospital. She'd taken off at a run and hopped into her car, breaking every speed limit posted to get to him. She'd been at his side in the hospital when he'd died. His last words to her were *I made a mistake. Don't trust him.*

She'd never figured out what his mistake was or who she couldn't trust. Both questions had haunted her.

Going back into the hospital after Jared's disappearance had nearly put her into a tailspin. Fran prided herself on keeping her cool at all times, but that day, she'd come close to having a panic attack in the hospital elevator. It had taken all her courage and years of training to tamp the anxiety down and complete her job.

She hated hospitals.

"Notifying Chief Spencer as well," Leslie announced, her voice accompanied by the sound of clicking keys.

Fran settled in to wait, scanning the area for any signs of whoever had left Jared here, in her yard. Poor kid.

Crack!

A bullet smashed into the ground at her feet.

Fran choked back a scream and burst to her feet. Dashing to the house, one of her sandals flew off her foot. She stumbled. Righting herself, she left the shoe and hobbled awkwardly up her steps. A second bullet smashed her abandoned mug when she ran past. Some of the shards hit the porch and others landed on the grass. Tea dripped from the railing.

Fran crashed into her house and slammed the door, leaning against it. Over the roar of her heartbeat, she heard Leslie yelling. Her hand still clutched her phone. "I'm okay, Leslie, but someone was shooting at me!"

"Stay in the house and lock all the doors. Help is on the way."

Bolting the front door, she ran to the back and repeated the process. Shaking so hard her teeth chattered, she returned to the living room and crouched behind the overstuffed recliner, her back pressed up against the wall. No one peering in the windows would be able to see her tucked into her hiding place.

A few minutes later, an engine purred on the driveway.

"Leslie," she whispered into the phone, "there's a car on my driveway."

"Hold on." More clicking of keys. Then she heard Leslie's voice. "Fran hears a car in her driveway. She's barricaded inside her house."

"Tell her it's me. I'm parked outside her front door."

"Fran, I have Dane on the line."

"I heard him. I'm on my way out now." She stood from her hiding place and strode to the closet. She needed real footwear. Shoving her bare feet into tall rubber boots, she made her way back out to the front porch. The coroner's SUV was a welcome sight.

Sirens shrilled up the long driveway then two Sutter Springs Police Department cruisers arrived. She relaxed when her friend Lieutenant Kathy Bartlett unfolded her lanky frame from behind the wheel of the first vehicle. No more bullets rained down, so she hoped the danger had passed. Kathy and the two officers from the second cruiser began to search the yard. When they waved that the area was clear, Dane Lenz, the coroner, exited his vehicle and headed over to the body.

Fran left the porch and made her way to Dane's side, shivering. She should have grabbed a coat. Between the rain and the shock of being used for target practice, she was chilled to the bone. Wrapping her arms around herself, she tightened her jaw to keep her teeth from chattering. They chattered anyway. Neither she nor Dane spoke. They arrived at the body and he immediately went to work. She remained near enough to answer questions, but not so close that she interfered with his duties.

The next moment, her muscles tightened again when a fourth vehicle slid in behind the coroner's.

A tall beanpole of a man exited. Piercing blue eyes glanced at her from behind wire-rimmed glasses. A Pittsburgh Pirates baseball cap covered his shocking copper hair, worn slightly longer than military length in a messy fade. His immaculate grooming highlighted the sharp lines of his jaw. Although he'd completed his training and could have probably grown a short beard, the most she'd ever seen on him was a five-o'clock after a long day's work, and that was once years ago. He'd always sported the clean-cut look.

FBI Special Agent Tanner Hall. He'd worked with Sean on several cases in the past, but Fran had never met him until he'd come to Sutter Springs on a case two years ago. She'd done her best to avoid him. His presence had been too painful for her.

But she'd never forgotten him. Would he know who her husband had warned her about? She'd never asked. What if she didn't like what he said about Sean? She liked to think he was on the side of good. But what if he wasn't?

If he was at the scene of this crime, it must mean the FBI had an interest in it. It couldn't be a coincidence that he showed up at the scene where the body of a missing youth had been discovered. How had he gotten there so fast? Would working with him give her the opportunity to answer the questions that kept her awake at night?

* * *

Tanner's gaze clashed with Francesca Brown's and his stomach tightened. She looked the same as he remembered, although with her hair plastered against her head and the way her amber eyes stared at him, she reminded him of puppy who'd been kicked and had learned to be wary. Briefly, his mind flashed to the images of the pictures that had littered Sean's desk and shelves. In most of them, she'd been laughing, her lovely face alight with joy.

He saw none of that vibrancy now. Shaking his head, he brought his focus back to the matter at hand.

Someone had shot at her. The broken ceramic cup on the porch could so easily have been her, the dark liquid seeping off the railing, her blood. She had come so close to being killed.

He forced his mind away from such thoughts. She was fine, just cold. Her late husband had been a colleague and a friend. He'd want Tanner to look out for his wife and put the criminal behind bars where he couldn't harm her. Thoughts of Sean always made him feel guilty. Tanner hadn't figured out that Sean was a target in time to save him. He promised himself he wouldn't fail again.

He'd seen too many people he knew injured or killed in the past fifteen years. Some people got used to the loss. Tanner never did.

Fran turned her head and her eyes met his. He searched them for signs of shock. She shivered, and her olive-toned skin was unnaturally pale, but she appeared to be holding her own.

When her eyes cut from him to watch the coroner approach, he sighed. A couple of years ago, he'd been in the area and had asked her out to dinner. Not romantically. Just because he'd been a colleague of her husband's and felt bad that he'd never taken the time to get to know the woman his good friend had married. She'd been polite in her refusal but had made it clear she wanted no part of anyone from Sean's past. He'd shrugged and accepted her position with minimal regret. Sometimes you had to give people space. Although he hoped it wouldn't make it awkward to work together now.

What she didn't know was that Jared Murray had been spotted alive several days ago. His sighting had reopened a federal case, and Tanner's boss, the special agent in charge, or the SAC for short, had assigned Tanner to take point, as he was already in the area. Now Jared had showed up dead on Francesca Brown's lawn.

When he'd heard that shots had been fired, nothing would have kept him away. At some point, he'd need to have a real conversation with her. While he didn't want to pain her, he'd become convinced that Sean had been murdered. What he didn't know, and what he hoped his late colleague's widow could shed some light on, was why a good man had been targeted and run down in the middle of the day on a busy street.

Tanner strode across the yard, waterlogged earth squishing beneath his hard-soled black shoes.

He squatted next to the coroner, a foot from where Fran stood in faded jeans and sparkly pink rubber boots. Removing his gaze from her legs, he refocused on the dead body in front of him.

"Cause of death?"

Dane Lenz glanced up. He was an older man with the face of a storyteller. Right now, harsh lines carved his skin on either side of his mouth. Tanner had met him two years earlier.

"Stab wounds. Multiple." Dane lifted aside the jacket

the young man wore to display his bloody T-shirt. Tanner sighed.

"He's been missing for a long time," Fran murmured, her voice like warm butter.

Tanner hesitated. They were law enforcement. And Jared no longer needed to hide. "Actually, he hasn't been missing. At least, not like you think."

"Explain, please."

He met her eyes. "You remember his father was arrested for involvement in arms dealing?"

She nodded, her amber eyes wide. "Right. When the police searched his car after his attack, trying to find some indication of who assaulted him and kidnapped Jared, they found evidence linking the judge to illegal activities. I remember pitying the poor wife. She left town soon after that."

He nodded. "Right. What no one knew at the time was that Jared hadn't been kidnapped. When they got a flat tire, Jared got out to change it. He was at the back of the car, bent down, when the men approached. They didn't see him. He heard what they were saying about his dad and realized his father had been a participant in several gun-related deaths. He hid under the car until the men had left, and then called the police. As a key witness, he was taken into federal custody and put into protective care. Both Jared and his mother were given new identities. After his mother disappeared a few months ago, he took off and stopped calling his handler. We're still trying to determine why he left. Did he get tired of the Witness Protection Program, or was he searching for his mom? Or did he have other reasons?"

She nodded. Fran had been a forensic sketch artist since she was twenty-five. He knew she'd been in the field for nearly ten years and was aware that sometimes the safety of the people they protected meant details were sealed.

"Hold on a minute. We need a drawing." Fran ran back in the house and returned with a sketchpad and a thick graphite pencil. She stood near the steps, sketching. Of course, a crime scene sketch. Many departments didn't have the resources to include a crime scene sketch. But none would turn down a drawing to supplement any photos. While photos captured a chunk of the scene at a time, a drawing was a scaled representation of all the known parts. Done well, a labeled illustration would allow those viewing it to see the relationship between objects, such as structures, weapons or blood spatter, and help to create a timeline. They also were invaluable during interviews as it gave the viewer access to all known factors at once.

Kathy Bartlett approached her. Tanner pushed himself to his feet and joined them. The police lieutenant nodded at him.

Fran ignored his presence, the tip of her tongue caught between her teeth as she completed the drawing. "There." She held out the sketchpad. It was a typical crime scene drawing. Nothing fancy. Just lines for the perimeter of the yard. She had identified where Jared had been found and put in points for where the two bullets had landed.

"We are finished with the preliminary search." Kathy took the drawing for a moment and snapped a picture of it with her phone. "I've called in the CSU to come and do an intensive sweep."

Ohio's crime scene unit would canvas the area more thoroughly.

Fran sighed. "I should probably dress and come into the station. I don't want to be here while they do that. And I have some sketches I need to complete anyway."

Tanner took a second glance at the sketch. "How close were you when that mug shattered?"

He hadn't meant to ask that. But his mind couldn't get past the image of her taking a bullet and bleeding out on the porch. He didn't know how Jared came to be on her front lawn. But he knew that Jared and Sean had met in connection with the judge's case. Jared's appearance here couldn't have happened by chance.

"I was only a few inches away. Had I not tripped on my sandal coming off, I might have been hit." Fran's voice remained steady, but the corners of her lips tightened. She might try to hide it, but it had shaken her.

Tanner swallowed hard. She'd come too close to death.

The smile she aimed at Kathy was the first sign of true warmth he'd ever seen from her. But he knew from Sean's picture collection that she hid a deeper, warmer side. What would it take to bring that side back into the open again?

Why was it his business anyway? He was there to work a case, not to play counselor to his late friend's widow.

Tanner assisted Dane with loading the stretcher and carrying Jared to the coroner's vehicle. He felt a little bruised emotionally. Jared had been a kid when he'd met him. A sweet boy most of the time, but he'd had his belligerent moments. Most teens did. Still, when he'd taken off, it had come as a complete shock.

Dane used the turnaround built into the top corner of the drive and headed out. He passed two SUVs on their way in. Tanner recognized the woman driving the first vehicle and nodded at her. She nodded back. When she parked, she and her team exited and began putting on gloves and taking their tools out to begin the search.

The crime scene unit arrived. Tanner returned to Fran and Kathy. They had stopped chatting and were watching the growing number of people moving about. Fran's expression became grimmer each moment. At least the rain had slowed to a light drizzle.

"I'm going to clean up and get ready to leave." Fran turned and went into the house without meeting his eyes again. It didn't appear to be deliberate avoidance. The woman's focus was legendary.

"Since he's a federal witness, this is all linked to a federal case. I need to be kept in the loop at all times," he informed Kathy.

Unlike her friend, Kathy smiled at him. "I get it. Jack and Nicole will be happy to see you."

Jack Quinn used to be his partner. That was before he'd married Lieutenant Nicole Dawson and they'd started a family. He had left the Bureau to head a department in a nearby security office. Some days, Tanner wondered if his friend hadn't made a better choice than he had.

The smile dwindled from her face. "I am sorry about Jared. He's so young."

Twenty-three was young.

"I need to know what Jared got involved with. Or who."

"Lieutenant!"

They pivoted to face the woman calling out. She was near the thick hedges in the corner of the yard. "We have something."

Kathy and Tanner strode over to where she stood.

"What do you have, Brenda?" he asked.

The crime scene investigator parted the bush with her latex-gloved hand, uncovering an open backpack. Inside the backpack, they saw clothes, protein bars and several bottles of water. And a toy horse. Jared had been a city dweller. He'd never been interested in horses, not even as a child. There was no reason for him to have a toy horse in his bag. Not if he had been traveling alone.

"Does that mean what I think it means?" Kathy demanded in a hoarse whisper.

Tanner took over. "We act like it does." He raised his voice and called out to the rest of the team roaming around the property. "Okay, people. There might be a second victim. Possibly a child."

The murmur of voices hushed and all the faces looking at him grew grim. It was bad enough knowing a young man had been murdered. It was even worse knowing they might be searching for the body of a child. The searchers set out, their shoulders and jaws set. If there was any hope of finding a child alive, every law enforcement officer would scour each inch of the grounds. It might take a while. Fran's front yard was an acre, if not a little more.

The screen door squeaked. Fran stepped onto the porch. She watched the proceedings for five seconds before she descended the stairs and moved to his side. The light floral scent of her shampoo tickled his nose. He had no doubt that she'd approached him only because he was closer to the house than Kathy. She'd never showed any preference for his company before.

"What's going on? Everyone looks intense. Has something happened?"

He nodded, unsurprised. As a forensic artist, Fran had honed her observation skills. Details such as the change in postures, tensions and facial expressions wouldn't escape her notice.

"Unfortunately, yes. The crime scene unit discovered a backpack with a toy in it. We think there may be a child around here."

He hadn't said "a body" on purpose. Tanner wanted to

retain hope, as unlikely as it was, until it was proved futile. He'd seen a lot of evil in his career, but he'd also seen some good. He chose to hope.

Fran's hands flew to her mouth. Giving him a single nod, she left his side and joined in the search. Every set of eyes helped.

While he explored, he sent up a silent prayer for help. He hadn't been a praying man very long. In fact, it wasn't until Jack had married and told him how his faith had helped him heal from his sister's death that Tanner had given faith more than a passing consideration. Lately, though, he'd started to see God's hand in his life.

His prayer was raw, and it wasn't fancy, but in his heart, he knew God heard him.

Questions raced through his mind. Why would Jared have been with a child? And how had he ended up here, on Fran's front lawn? And why had someone shot at Fran? How was she connected with his case?

TWO

No matter how often Fran saw the horrible acts humanity was capable of, it always shocked her when children were involved. Maybe it hit her so hard because she and Sean had suffered a devastating loss right before his loss.

"Tanner!" she called out.

"Yeah?" He jogged over, those long legs carrying him to her side so fast, she blinked. "You find something?"

She shook her head. "No. But I am wondering if we should search the area in backyard too?"

"We will," Brenda called from across the lawn. "You have two and a half acres, plus there is a field on the other side of your property. We'll search this area then spiral out."

She nodded, familiar with this pattern of exploration in a widening circle. It was often used in large outdoor settings when there was much ground to cover. Glad that she had exchanged her casual shoes for more durable footwear, she bent her head and continued to assist in the pursuit.

She'd never been involved in a search before. She suspected if it weren't for the urgency of a child's life at risk, she would have been asked to keep out of the way. Regardless of her connection with law enforcement, she wasn't a police officer, and her training had not involved the correct manner to process a crime scene. She rarely saw this side of the operation.

Finding nothing in the front yard, the search expanded to the sides and back of the house. It was a large structure with a great deal of land, some of the land in the back had been allowed to overgrow to provide a barrier between her house and the neighbors'. Not that she had a problem with her neighbors. They seemed like a nice young couple. But they had only lived there for about six months, and Fran was an introvert by nature, so she hadn't gone out of her way to introduce herself to them.

The rain stopped about twenty minutes into the search. As often happened in early autumn in the Midwest, the coolness ushered in with the precipitation faded when the clouds blew away and the sun beat down upon them. Within an hour, the temperature had risen to seventy-four degrees and the humidity levels were off the chart. Fran could practically feel the water droplets in the air.

Soon, she removed her light sweater and tied it around her waist. Then she continued in her cotton blouse, thankful she had selected one with small fluttery-capped sleeves rather than a long-sleeved or quarter-sleeved blouse. Already, sweat bubbled her neck and back.

The search pattern reached the outside of her property. Fran began to lose any hope that they would find the child alive. Not that she'd had much to begin with. It had been nearly two hours since she'd opened her front door and spotted Jared's shoes pointing to the sky. Would a young child be able to hide for that long, silently, unless he or she were injured or worse?

Not that they knew for sure a child was there. They had a suspicion, but so far, no actual proof. This might all be a total waste of time.

She would far prefer that than the alternative.

Her stomach grumbled and her throat felt like she'd tried to swallow a wad of cotton. Fran didn't complain. She ignored her discomfort. It was unimportant at the moment. What was a little hunger to saving a life?

"I found him!" an officer called out. Perry, she recalled. "He's alive, but traumatized."

Relief swept the team in a visible flood. Fran saw a wave of shoulders relaxing. They gathered around Perry, some slapping his back in congratulations as they crowded around the little boy sitting among the tall grass. He rocked back and forth, his knees pulled up to his chest with his thin arms wrapped around them. The child appeared to be about five years old. He was dressed in a pair of sweatpants and T-shirt, but she didn't think they were his clothes. His hair had a very unique cut to it, similar to those worn by the Amish children in the area. In addition, he repeated some words that she was fairly certain weren't English. They had a hard sound, like German. Or Pennsylvania Dutch.

The group around him tightened, edged in closer. His rocking increased. He clapped his hands over his ears and made several high keening sounds. The hair on the nape of her neck rose.

Brenda pushed her way through to the front of the group. With the confident air of a mother, she charged forward. The child shrank back from her open arms and his keening increased. He swayed back and forth, his eyes skittering to the side, never making eye contact.

She watched Brenda edge closer.

Suddenly, something clicked in her mind. She knew if Brenda tried to hug him, it would be disastrous. Without thinking of how uncomfortable she was to be the center of attention, Fran shoved herself past the people blocking her way.

"Wait! Brenda! Don't touch him!"

All gazes switched from the child to Fran.

Brenda froze, scanning the area. "What's wrong? I don't see anything dangerous."

Fran continued forward, keeping her movements and voice calm and nonthreatening.

"It's not dangerous. Watch him. See the way he's rocking to calm himself? And listen to his words. Between the noises he's making, he's repeating the same sequence of words over and over. Pretty sure they're Amish words. Every time we get closer, his rocking increases. I think he may be a child with autism."

The group stopped moving. She felt some of the tension return and understood it. The poor little boy needed help. How were they to help him if they could not get close to him?

And how were they to find his family? Had his parents reported him missing? And if they had, was the child from the area?

Fran stepped to Brenda's side to observe the child more closely. He tensed then looked at her blouse.

"Stars," he murmured.

She glanced down. The shirt she'd worn had tiny stars embroidered all over it in a shimmery gold thread. It was one of her favorites. Carefully, she stooped lower to the child. He didn't so much as glance at her face but continued to look at the stars. When he began to speak, she realized he was counting them. Her niece, who had been diagnosed with autism when she was three, did something similar.

Brenda squatted next to her. Immediately, he shrank back.

"Hey. It's okay." Fran stretched out a hand almost in slow

motion. When he didn't react, she touched his arm. He let her touch him, raising his fingers to trace the stars on her shoulder. "I'm going to try and carry him. Maybe we can get him to the station."

She couldn't drive, that was clear. She aimed a pointed glance at Tanner.

"I'll drive you," Tanner said, taking her hint. "You can sit in the back seat with our little friend."

No one protested. Fran slowly reached out and wrapped her arms around the child, waiting for a shriek to blast her eardrums. He didn't make any sounds to indicate he was upset, merely continued to count the stars on her shirt. When he snuggled in a little closer, she glanced down. He wasn't being cuddly but was so intrigued by her stars that he let her hold him.

One of the crime scene members asked if they should bring her the horse.

Brenda frowned and shook her head. "As much as I would love to give it to him, everything inside that backpack needs to be photographed and tagged as evidence. If he loves horses, and if we can't find his family immediately, I might ask the chief if we could buy him one to comfort him."

His fascination with Fran's starry shirt definitely wouldn't last too long. They needed to find something for him that would hold his attention.

"That seems reasonable. Let's get him out of this hot sun." Tanner jerked his thumb toward his vehicle.

Brenda and another officer helped her to feet. She thanked them and followed Tanner to his SUV. He opened the back passenger door for her but stopped her before she stepped in. "It'll be safer for him in the back seat. Wait a few seconds, though. Let it cool for a moment. The seats are leather and could be hot."

She nodded, somewhat surprised by his demeanor. Two years ago, she'd had the chance to see him in action when he and his former partner, Jack Quinn, had showed up to assist in a case revolving around child abduction and murder. He had struck her as a bit overzealous, but very efficient and competent. Tanner did his job well, but he excelled at collecting and interpreting data. It had impressed her, but it had also been too reminiscent of Sean and his love of numbers. Fran had immediately put the brakes on any stirring interest. When he'd asked her out for dinner, she'd known he'd asked as her husband's colleague. But she hadn't been able to accept. Her pain over her husband's death had been only a few years old, and meeting someone who'd reminded her of Sean had been overwhelming.

Seeing Tanner in action today, Fran admitted she had misjudged the handsome special agent. He was comfortable taking command of a situation, which shy Sean could never have done. Tanner had included her in the conversation without hesitation, never treating her as anything less than an equal. While Sean had respected her and her career choice, he had tended to view forensic sketch artists as a dying breed, preferring to rely on technology. They'd had more than one argument over his certainty that she needed to develop other skills for when, not if, her job became obsolete. It had always put her on the defensive when her husband had insisted she'd chosen a career with no future. Although she'd known he hadn't meant to be insulting, she'd always been left with the feeling of being less than equal. Not a feeling she appreciated.

She recalled Tanner's speed when he'd run up to her. He was also more active than Sean had ever been.

Fran shook her head, distraught. What was she doing? Sean had been an excellent husband and she'd loved him unconditionally. To stand there and compare him with another man felt disloyal. And it broke her heart to admit Sean had been lacking in any way. At the end of the day, for all his faults, he'd been her husband, and she'd promised to love him until death parted them. That death had come far sooner than expected didn't lesson the depth of her commitment.

"Go ahead and get in now." Tanner was at her elbow, speaking in a low voice. "Watch your head."

Nodding, she ducked into the back seat as slowly as possible. She didn't want to disturb the child. Gingerly, she sat on the edge of the leather seat then scooted back. "We don't have a child seat."

"Do you think he'd tolerate one?"

"I doubt it. If he's Amish, he's possibly never been in one before. The restraints might scare him." She glanced down at the child. He had slumped against her. "He's asleep."

"We need to go. No telling when or where that shooter will show up again."

"Even with all these people about?"

"Let's not take any chances."

She pulled the seat belt over herself and the boy, taking care to put the shoulder strap behind her. This might keep them from flying forward, but that strap could strangle him or snap his neck.

"Ready," she said.

"I'll drive slowly. But I'm very concerned about how long he might have been out in the weather. His skin looks pale to me."

"Yeah. I read a book once by an expert in the field of autism. She stressed that people with autism could be overly sensitive to light, color and sound. He may not like to be outdoors in sunlight." She carefully readjusted her legs to get as comfortable as possible without disturbing the child. "But we have no way of knowing if it's our imagination or his true shade."

"That's one problem."

He closed her door, taking care not to slam it, then moved to the front and got inside the SUV and started the engine. Thankfully, the FBI kept their vehicles in tip-top condition. It would be a nightmare if his had roared like a dinosaur when started. Tanner skillfully backed up, turned the vehicle around and drove down the driveway. At the road, he waited for a passing car before heading toward town.

"Where should we go first?" Tanner asked. She was gratified he'd asked for her input, well aware he could make any and all decisions on his own.

She dreaded going to the hospital, but told herself to deal with it. This child had to come before her own selfish wishes.

"I thought about the hospital, but I am worried about it. Would all the bright lights disturb him? And if we have to wait in the emergency room waiting area, he might have trouble handling it." Fran bit her lip. So would she, but she wasn't about to say that out loud.

"I don't know that much about autism, so I'll follow your lead on this."

Fran glanced his way. "Maybe we should go to the station. I could call Chief Spencer and clear out a conference room. If we keep the lights low, maybe we can get a doctor to attend us there."

"That sounds like a plan."

"What about Children Services?" She hated to think of letting him go with strangers. But what choice did they have?

"We can call them from the station."

Her gaze dropped to the child in her arms. "Where are your mommy and daddy, sweetie? How do we find them?"

Tanner heard Fran's murmured comments. His chest tightened. He'd wondered the same thing. It was hard enough for a child who could communicate with those around them. For one with special needs, a situation like this had to be terrifying. How much did the child understand?

What had Jared been doing with the boy? Was he part of some nefarious plot, or had Jared been a victim, the same as the boy in the back? He couldn't see Jared hurting the child. When Jared had first joined the program, he'd revealed the extent of his father's crimes. The judge had no problem selling guns to gangs and cartels. Even when two of the guns he'd sold to gangs in the United States were linked to drive-by shootings, resulting in eight deaths, two of them children under thirteen, he hadn't stopped.

Jared had been devastated to learn his father had been responsible for children being hurt. All for money. He didn't know what had happened or why Jared had left the WIT-SEC program, but he'd do his best to discover the facts.

Tanner wanted justice for the boy who'd been robbed of his opportunity to become an adult and reach his potential.

He skirted around the next corner, keeping both hands on the wheel. The two-lane road Fran lived on constantly twisted and turned, reminding him more of a roller coaster than a roadway. Give him a straight highway any day rather than one like this with more curves than a pretzel.

"How's he doing back there?" he called out. He genuinely wanted to know. He also admitted the silence was a bit unnerving. Tanner liked noise. The hum of computers or music pouring from the speakers. He'd gotten used to being surrounded by sound in his work and in his time to relax. This thick silence wrapping around them made his skin itch.

Plus, Fran had a lovely voice, low and smooth. He wondered idly what her singing voice was like then rolled his eyes at his own random thoughts.

"He's still asleep. I worry about what happens when I change my shirt. This is my only one with stars on it."

He nodded. "I hope he's built up a connection with you. You're the only one he would let touch him."

"I don't think this has to do with me. I think it had to do with his finding something that snagged his attention and kept it. He likes to count." Her voice was thoughtful.

"So keep wearing clothes with patterns he can count."

She snorted softly.

Even that sound was attractive. He grinned at his own ridiculousness.

"You know," she murmured, "autistic children sometimes have trouble making connections with others. They see the world in a unique way. I'm not saying they can't have relationships, just that they take more effort to develop."

"I didn't know that." He paused, wondering if he should ask personal questions. "I don't mean to pry—and feel free to tell me to mind my own business—but why do you know so much about autism?"

She didn't answer at first. Afraid he'd pushed the boundaries too far, he glanced back at her. The sadness in her face made him swallow. "I know because my younger sister's daughter has autism. She recently turned eight."

He'd always thought she was an only child. "You have a sister? I had no idea."

How could he have worked with Sean for so long and

not have known this? What else had his old friend not told him? He didn't like the direction his thoughts were going.

"I'm guessing by your reaction my husband never talked about my family. That's fair." Her chuckle was rife with bitterness and pain. "My parents are very old-fashioned. You could probably guess that, with a name like Francesca."

He smiled into the rearview mirror at her. "I've never met another Francesca. I like it. It suits you. I actually prefer it to Fran."

This time, her soft laugh held genuine amusement. "I've not heard that before. Anyway, my folks didn't approve of Sean. My family had wealth and my mother had always imagined I'd marry a neurosurgeon or something like that. I remember when I started dating Sean, she'd always try to set me up on dates with the 'right' sort of young men. A forensic accountant wasn't good enough for Barbara and Edward Warren. When I defied them and married him anyway, they stopped talking to us. I thought they'd grow used to my marriage and change their minds, but they never did. My sister, Anastasia, used to be the only one who wanted anything to do with me. Until she got married. I guess her husband isn't that different from my parents. I wasn't even at their wedding. She wanted me there but said it would be easier if I wasn't. When he went away on business, we used to get together. Then he found out and put an end to it. It's been five years since I've seen her or Lucy, my niece."

Wow. He couldn't even imagine. How could you not invite your only sibling to your wedding?

"I don't know what to say." He paused. "I know this isn't my place to judge, but that relationship seems unhealthy."

"I agree. But what can I do? She's an adult."

"I don't have any answers for you."

"Let's not talk about my dysfunctional family. What about you? Do you have any brothers or sisters?"

He almost felt guilty after hearing about her family. "Well, yeah. I have three brothers and two sisters. I'm the oldest. Then there's Zachary, Logan, Lillian, Sebastian and the baby of the family, Vanessa."

In the mirror, he saw her shake her head. "Six children! You must have had a very loud house."

"Yep. Probably more so than a house with only two girls." His mom had never complained about the noise. Both his parents seemed to thrive on the chaos. He'd been the one who'd needed order. He was also the one who'd run from God when his brother had nearly died from cancer. Zach had survived but would forever be scarred by the experience. It had devastated him when he'd discovered that the chemo had deprived him of the ability to one day father children. And then, three years ago, when Zach had finally met someone he could love, cancer had struck again. His fiancée bailed on him, leaving him with a bitter attitude and no fiancée. At thirty-four, his brother had survived more than most people would in a lifetime.

Tanner hadn't come to terms with why someone like Zach had had to suffer.

He sighed. He didn't want to disrupt the positive vibes flowing. Plus, they were in the middle of a rather delicate situation. But they might not get another time to speak privately. If anyone had the right to know his suspicions, it was the beautiful woman in the car with him.

"Look, Fran, there's something I need to tell you, and I'm afraid it might come as a bit of a shock."

He felt more than saw her straightening up in the back seat.

"Go on."

Tanner flinched. All the warmth had drained from her tone, leaving it guarded and chilly.

"It's about today's situation. It's odd, don't you think? I can't prove anything. Not yet. But I don't like coincidences."

"Neither do I."

That was good, but he wasn't sure if she knew where he was going with this. "I just think it's strange that Jared appeared on your lawn. He had worked very closely with Sean and me. Why your lawn?"

"I didn't know Sean knew him too."

"He did. He was our numbers man. The judge had been on our radar for a while. Sean was looking into his personal finances. I didn't think it at the time, but over the past few years, I've become convinced that there was more to your husband's death than a simple hit and run. We were at a critical point in our investigation."

"You think he was murdered," she said, a slight hiccough-like catch in her voice.

"I do."

"Oh." She sighed.

He risked a look in her direction. Tears sparkled on her lashes, but her expression radiated relief. "You look almost glad I think he was murdered."

He didn't mean to sound accusatory. It just wasn't the reaction he'd expected.

"I am. Tanner, I've been wondering if his accident was more than that for years. He'd been super stressed the weeks leading up to his death. Whenever I asked about it, he'd say it was work stuff and clamp down."

"I'm sorry he couldn't tell you more."

"Well, I always wondered if he wouldn't talk to me because he was angry with me."

He definitely didn't want to hear this. But, if he was

going to get to the bottom of things, he sort of needed to be intrusive and find out everything that he could about Sean's last moments. "I'm sorry, Fran. I don't want to intrude—"

"But you need to know what was going on," she stated flatly. "We hadn't told anyone about it, but I'd recently miscarried."

"I'm sorry. I know that doesn't help, but I am."

"Sean felt it was my fault because I'd been grocery shopping two days before and someone rear-ended me."

He blinked. "How is that your fault?"

"You got me. But he said if I had gone straight home, it wouldn't have happened, and I wouldn't have lost the baby. The doctor told us the car accident did not cause the miscarriage, but Sean insisted it did. And when I told him I was following our normal weekly schedule, that I always grocery shopped on Saturday after my coffee date with Kathy, he was adamant I'd been in the wrong."

That didn't sound like the logical man Tanner had worked with. Something else must have been going on. He kept the thought to himself. He needed time to digest what he'd learned to see if he could come up with any reasonable explanations.

Glancing in the rearview mirror, all the questions in his mind fled. The car behind them was following way too close. Dangerously close. Sitting straighter, he pressed down on the gas. The engine revved and his SUV picked up speed.

The vehicle behind them sped up as well.

"Hey, Fran. I think we're being followed."

She swallowed. "What do we do?"

He thought for a moment. "If I slow down, maybe you can get out and I'll lead the driver away…"

"Not. I doubt that would work. How would I travel with him?" She jerked her head to indicate the child. "He probably won't react well and I'd literally be carrying a child having a tantrum. We'll have to make it to the police station."

"We might not have a choice," he ground out.

The treacherous road curved around again. He didn't like going so fast when he had passengers without safety seats. "Slide into the floorboard."

She unbuckled and removed the straps, tipping forward to untangle from the one behind her shoulder. Then she took the child and slid down to the ground.

He said a prayer that the child would remain sleeping. If he didn't, and tried to fight, not only would it distract Tanner, but it would leave the child more vulnerable.

A bullet crashed through the back window.

The driver behind them was out for blood. Who was the target? If Tanner didn't find a way out, they'd all become the next victims.

THREE

Glass showered the back seat of the SUV. Tanner risked a quick look at the passenger-side floorboard to verify neither Fran nor the child had been injured. She hunched over the little boy, using her body as a shield to protect him. Tanner saw no blood and released the breath he'd been holding. The boy was cocooned in her arms. His eyes popped open, and he arched his back like a cat trying to escape an unwanted embrace. A high-pitched howl erupted from him. Tanner gritted his teeth and focused his attention on the road, doing his best to elude their attacker.

"No, no, no." The child began to chant, each word louder than the next.

"Hand me your jacket," Fran called up to him.

Tanner grabbed his jacket off the passenger seat and tossed it back to her. She latched on to it and dragged it around the little boy's shoulders. In the side mirror, something flashed. Tanner swerved the SUV to the other lane, which was thankfully free of any oncoming traffic, just in time to avoid the second bullet. When he spotted a truck rounding the bend, he veered back into his own lane. The car had ventured past the middle line, and narrowly escaped being slammed by the truck, whose driver gave a long burst of his horn to warn them to stay on their own side.

Something fell to the asphalt. The wheels of the large oncoming vehicle rolled over it, leaving a trail of smashed pieces in its wake. Their tail had dropped his gun. Now it was useless. Tanner muttered a quick prayer of thanks. That truck driver might be annoyed at the moment, but his appearance had very likely saved their lives.

Not that he had any expectation that the gunman behind them would give up that easily.

Had Tanner not had Fran and the child with him, he might have been tempted to do something dangerous. But he couldn't risk it. Protecting those in his care must be his primary objective.

Behind him, Fran's calm voice tried to comfort the boy. He caught a glimpse of her wrapping his coat around the child, almost swaddling him. Then she began to rock him. Amazingly, it seemed to soothe him. Partially. His volume decreased, although he continued to cry, "No!"

Fran started counting, spacing the numbers out evenly. "One, two, three." The youngster gave an angry little sob then his crying dwindled. Tanner risked a look back. While the child made no attempt to meet her eyes or engage with her, his entire posture suggested he was listening to the monotonic recitation of numbers. By the time she reached eight, the boy was counting with her.

They took another curve. The rubber tires hit the rumble strip on the shoulder, creating a loud, low-pitched grinding sound. When the child paused, Fran's voice increased in volume. Tanner eased the SUV back onto the main part of the road.

The counting resumed at normal volume. They were up to twenty-two.

Lifting his gaze to the rearview mirror, he saw their attacker was still there. In fact, he was coming closer. Tanner put more pressure on the pedal, pushing it closer to the floor. The speed limit was forty-five. The speedometer hit fifty-five and kept climbing. And still the car kept up with them. Sweat broke out on his brow. Sixty. Sixty-five.

If he went any faster, they would fly right off the road and over the edge. It was a long drop down. He didn't know how far. All he could see were the tops of hundreds of trees lining the road. He tightened his grip on the wheel until his knuckles were white. His SUV was a top-notch vehicle, but evidently the vehicle chasing them was built for speed. Tanner knew what was coming. Around these curves, there was nowhere to maneuver and no open roads to turn on to evade him.

The vehicle zoomed closer. Tanner had no choice but to accelerate again. He hit the gas pedal, slamming it to the floor. His stomach lurched. Traveling this fast around the curves was asking for trouble. He didn't have any other options. The moment he exited the curve and could peel his right hand from the steering wheel, he hit the phone icon on the dashboard then slapped his hand back on the wheel. The SUV shimmied beneath him.

"Please state a command," the robotic voice ordered.

"Dial Chief Spencer," Tanner shouted. His habit of making sure the local law enforcement chief and agencies were on speed dial came in handy.

"Dialing."

The phone began to ring. Chief Mike Spencer answered.

Tanner cut him off. "I have Fran Brown and a child in my vehicle. We're being chased by an assailant on Hatch Road. We've traveled about six miles from Fran's house. I'm going too fast, if we go over, we'll be going down the ravine. But if I slow down, he'll catch us."

Maybe "ravine" was an exaggeration, but it was at least

a two-story drop. He doubted the guardrails would stop their fall.

"Does he have a weapon?"

"He did. He dropped it and it got destroyed. I have no idea if he has another. But he is going to hit us. I have no doubt of that."

The SUV jolted as his prediction came true.

Fran let out a small shriek. Then she immediately returned to counting. This time, a slight quaver betrayed her tension and fear.

Tanner kept control, but it was hard.

"He hit us, sir. I don't know how long we can keep this up."

"I'm sending help. Hold on."

He'd do his best, but he couldn't make any promises. He'd never driven in conditions like this before.

The car behind them punched into his bumper again. His SUV lurched, ripping the steering wheel from his hands. Tanner caught it and kept the vehicle on the road, but it was a close call. He had no options. He couldn't drive and shoot, and there was no place to turn back. The only thing he could do was to keep driving. Fran and the little boy continued to count in the back.

He caught the strain tightening her voice. She was keeping the child calm, but he knew it wasn't easy for her to ignore the stress of their situation. Any moment could be their last. The only positive was that the gunman was not shooting any more. Even if he had a second weapon he probably couldn't fire and keep up with them on these curves. If they could just hold on.

In the distance, he heard sirens coming toward them.

Would they make it in time? They were still too far away to see the flashing lights.

Another curve loomed ahead. This one seemed narrower and steeper than before. Tall trees jutted above the ridge, looking like they had grown out of nothing. A sign on the edge of the road read No Guardrail. Why would they not have a barrier between traffic and a drop into an abyss?

Behind him, the engine of their tail closing in revved.

"Hold on. He's coming again."

Tanner tried to steer the SUV toward the middle of the lane. At the last moment, an oncoming Jeep rounded the curve from the other direction, honking its horn. He jerked the SUV's wheel back and avoided smashing into it. His tires skidded on the shoulder. He clenched his jaw. Way too close to the edge for his comfort.

Their tail smashed into his bumper. This time, the SUV spun out of control. Tanner's stomach dropped. The tires left the pavement, and their vehicle flew over the edge of the ravine in a downward arc. Fran screamed. The child in her arms burrowed into her, howling.

There was nothing he could do as his SUV fell.

Fran had the sensation that her stomach had taken flight and was trying to leave her body, just like being on a roller coaster that had gone into a deep dive. But this time, there was no track or safety harness to keep them safe.

She didn't even have a seat belt, sitting on the floorboard.

She needed to protect the little boy shrieking in her arms. Flipping over, she adjusted their position so he was on the floor and she was balanced above him. Bracing her arms, she kept herself from pressing against him and smothering him. If they jolted wrong, her arms would break.

The poor thing was terrified. His piercing screams crashed around in her head. Still, she remained where she was. Maybe she wouldn't survive this, but hopefully he would. Tanner was yelling in the front seat, but Fran couldn't make out the words.

When the SUV shuddered to a halt, she flew off her charge, her head and back slamming against the roof of the vehicle. Before she could catch her breath, her body banged against the floor, becoming wedged between Tanner's seat and the middle seat. Tanner had his seat back so far to accommodate his long legs. The Amish boy huddled in the opposite wheel well, curled into a ball. It worried her how silent he was, but she could make out his side moving, so he continued to breathe. Tilting her head, she gazed out the window. Leaves and branches smashed flat against the glass.

They were in a tree. Her breath caught in her throat. When help arrived, how would they rescue them without tipping the SUV out of the tree it was nestled in and sending it tumbling to the ground below?

"Tanner," she called, her voice hoarse and her throat raw. She hadn't been aware of screaming, but she must have. There was no other explanation for why it felt like there were razor blades tearing at her throat when she talked. Pain was irrelevant. It meant she was still alive.

It worried her that there no was response from the man in the driver's seat. "Tanner?"

Fear trickled down her spine. Was he alive?

Groaning, she attempted to push herself out of the small space restricting her, feeling as if her skin were being rubbed away. She'd have some bruises and welts, but that was unimportant. Under her, the SUV shook and swayed. Fran froze in place. Sweat soaked the back of her neck, leaking through the thin material of her shirt. Despite the sultry heat of the day, she shivered and her teeth began to chatter.

Was she going into shock? She wasn't injured, but she knew a severe emotional trauma could have that effect. Well, being shot at, finding a dead body and a traumatized autistic child, then being forced off a road into a tree who knew how far off the ground could definitely be categorized as trauma.

On second thought, if she could manage sarcasm, she probably wasn't in shock. Just terrified.

But she was alive.

"Tanner?" She tried again.

To her relief, he responded with a low moan. She heard him shift his weight in his seat. The SUV shook again. Her stomach clenched.

"Don't move!" She hissed at him, as if speaking at a natural decibel level would cause them to tumble into space. "We're stuck in the trees."

"Better in the trees than all the way down." He groaned again. "My airbag deployed. I'm stuck here." His voice sounded muffled, as if he were speaking through a wad of cotton.

Fran stretched her neck out so she could see beyond the edge of the driver's seat. From where she crouched on the floorboard, she could barely make out the edges of the airbag bubbled around Tanner like it was hugging him.

"Is it blocking your breathing at all? Your voice sounds muffled."

"No. I can breathe fine. It's uncomfortable. The airbag's already starting to deflate." Indeed, each word was clearer than the previous one. He paused. "Not to worry you, but I'm pretty sure I have a cracked rib or two."

A chill ran through her. What if it was more than a cracked rib? What if he had internal bleeding? While they were stuck in this predicament, he could bleed out.

"Can you feel your legs?"

"Yeah. I'm fine. I just don't know how we're going to get ourselves out of this. How's the kid?"

She glanced over. "He's breathing. And he's rocking a little. But apparently not hard enough to shake your SUV."

"He's small. I doubt if he weighs forty pounds. Still." He paused. "I'm worried he might be hurt and we can't see it."

He started to move and the vehicle shook again, then jolted slightly, dipping forward, as if warning them not to do anything foolish. "Wow. I don't think that was a good idea."

She swallowed, her throat suddenly dry.

A sound like a tornado siren blared through the vehicle. She whelped in surprise. "Sorry. That's my phone," he said.

Carefully, his arm reached around the airbag and pushed the button to answer the call.

"Hello?"

"Tanner, it's Chief Spencer." A familiar, calming voice came from the SUV's speakers. "We're directly above you. Are you, the child or Fran injured?"

"Fran?"

"I think I'm okay."

"Fran says she'd fine. I think I might have injured my ribs. We're not sure about the boy. It's possible, but if he is, we don't know how severely. Sir, we can't move. Every time we even breathe too hard, this bucket of bolts shakes like it's ready to do a nosedive out of this tree. And we're pretty sure this Amish kid in here with us has autism. He seems to have bonded a little with Fran but neither of us can tell if he has any injuries or if he's just scared."

A burst of chatter from the other end answered them. The chief's voice came through the loudest. Everyone above was trying to figure out the best way to extricate them from their current situation.

"Alright, Tanner." The chief came back on the line, his tone as smooth as if they were chatting about going out for lunch. "We have a helicopter on the way. Hang tight for a few more minutes. We'll get you out."

Fran's heart raced. Her gut flipped like she'd swallowed a live fish that continued to flail inside her stomach. If their slightest movement upset the SUV, how would they get out?

Since Sean's death, her faith had taken a beating. She still believed in God, but doubt about Him as a loving Father had festered. Her prayer life had grown stale in the midst of the lukewarmness. She knew it was wrong, but she'd even shut herself off from her church family. She used to find such comfort in worship.

She clenched her hands together and prayed while a small voice in her mind taunted her, calling her hypocritical.

It was true, but she persevered in her fervent litany.

A loud chopping hum, like a thousand Canadian geese taking flight simultaneously, swooped overhead.

"If that thing flies too close, it could unbalance us," she whisper-yelled to Tanner, hyperaware of the little boy still rocking inches from where she crouched, her leg muscles beginning to cramp. She wouldn't be able to stand if she didn't move soon.

"They won't. Look. They are dropping a ladder."

A man clung to the rungs as the flexible line neared the passenger side of the SUV. Tanner hit all the window switches, lowering them. Fran glanced at the man and swallowed. How did they expect this to work?

"Tanner, you okay? Your eyes look irritated."

"I'm fine. I think it's from the gasses released by the airbag once it deflated. Not that I don't trust you, Gabe, but this is going to require some coordination."

"Yeah, I can see that. You might not like my idea."

"I have none, so let's hear it."

"I'm going to get Fran and the kid out. While I'm doing that, can you hang out your window to balance?"

"Wait! Won't the vehicle fall?" It was the most daredevil idea she'd ever heard.

"It shouldn't. It will rock, for sure. But this tree is huge, and the vehicle is wedged in a wide vee. The worst-case scenario is that it will tip forward, not sideways. If it does, you need to get out and hold on to the branches."

There was no other choice. At Gabe's gentle directions, she inched ahead, her frozen muscles protesting with every move. Tanner was slowly shifting his weight, pulling himself up through the window.

The SUV shuddered beneath them.

"Don't stop," Gabe ordered when she paused. "Trust me. You're doing fine."

She grabbed the coat still wrapped around the boy and started counting again. He stopped rocking then began counting, his words tumbling over hers, rushing her to count faster. She took him in her arms.

"Stars, one star, two star…" He began counting the stars on her shirt. When she tried to hand him to Gabe, he bellowed in her ear and held on tight.

"I'll have to do this."

"I'll hold on to you from the other side. Tanner, you get out when we do. I'll have to lower the rope back for you."

They were going to leave him.

Fran forced herself to breathe, knowing that if she hesitated, she might be condemning him to a painful death. Blocking out the shrieks as best she could, she held tight to the little one and allowed Gabe to drag her from the car.

It rocked and slid forward. He held her tight from the other side of the ladder.

"Tanner, get out!" Gabe yelled.

The SUV fell forward. It slid out of the crevice and crashed into the ground below. She jerked her head around. Where was Tanner? Had he gotten out, or had the sudden fall of the vehicle take him with it?

FOUR

Tanner gripped the thick branch with his arms and used his core muscles to pull himself on top of it. Thankfully, the limb was the almost equal to a medium-size trunk. It held his weight. Now all he had to do was stay there until Gabe sent the ladder back for him.

Lifting his eyes, he squinted. Too many leaves and branches in his way. All he saw was a sea of green. The constant drone of the helicopter and the lack of screaming reassured him. Even the kid wasn't hollering. His heart broke for the little boy.

Tanner didn't know that much about autism. He had heard that children with autism were more comfortable with routine. What had happened in the last day, or however long he'd been missing from his family, had to be the antithesis of the structure he needed to remain calm and happy.

Shifting his weight, Tanner crawled a foot toward the end of the branch, enabling himself to see through the foliage in time to watch Fran and the kid disappear inside the chopper.

Good. The worry that he'd allowed his friend's widow to die a horrible death was muted. Although it didn't completely disappear. While she was alive and, to his knowledge uninjured, they were far from out of the woods.

Whoever had forced them over the edge remained at large. Every instinct inside him shouted the villain would be back to finish what he'd started. Tanner intended to stand squarely in his path and shut him down before he managed to get to either Fran or the kid.

The big question returned. Who was the target? Surely, not the child. He looked like he was maybe four, five at the most. Tanner didn't know how much he communicated, although he'd counted and yelled "no" clearly.

The helicopter lowered and loomed directly above him. Sinuously, the ladder slid out and plopped next to him, swinging like it was tempting him to reach out and grab hold of it.

Tanner sat up, balancing his weight on the tree branch, and stretched both arms toward the ladder, wincing when his ribs protested the movement. Despite the pain, he kept moving. He could worry about his injuries once he was safely in the helicopter with Fran and the kid. Right now, he needed to focus on joining them so that they could get to the hospital, find who the kid belonged to and start searching for whoever had killed Jared and attempted to take out Fran. Fury clouded his vision momentarily.

Tanner vowed not to rest until the unsub who'd gone after that woman and child was behind bars, hopefully for the remainder of his natural life.

He shifted his weight off the steady branch and onto the shaky, shivering ladder. His stomach quailed in response. Briefly, the image of the ladder breaking under his weight floated through his brain. He scoffed at the idea. The ladder had held the weight of Gabe, Fran and a squirming child minutes ago. While Gabe was shorter than his own six-foot frame, where Tanner tended to be on the wiry side, the firefighter was burly and built like a linebacker. If the ladder could safely carry the others, it could hold Tanner as he climbed. They were built to withstand over nine hundred pounds. However, some fears were not rational.

He'd had a problem with unsteady surfaces ever since he was a kid and had taken a dare to run full speed across a rickety wooden bridge. The swaying structure hadn't bothered him at all until the bridge had collapsed under him and he'd fallen twenty feet to the water below, breaking his right leg and his left wrist and nearly drowning in the process. Since then, he'd avoided shaky surfaces and large bodies of moving water whenever possible. Squeezing his eyes shut for a second, he banished that memory. He didn't have time for it.

Tanner wasn't a vain man, but he prided himself on his ability to remain calm and logical in tricky circumstances.

Setting his mind to the task before him, he began to ascend the wobbly ladder. Putting one hand over the other, he carefully closed each fist around the rungs and moved up, keeping his pace consistent. Sliding his feet onto the rungs terrified him, but he didn't stop. Maybe it would have been easier if he had looked down to see where his feet were going, but there was no way he could do that and hold his breakfast in.

The last thing he needed was to let these phobias take charge of him. Tanner had grown skilled at working through his fears.

It felt like an hour by the time he finally arrived at the top and Gabe and another man dragged him inside the helicopter.

Gauging by the expressions on their faces, however, it hadn't taken him nearly as long as he'd feared. Gabe gave a quiet command to the pilot. The helicopter rose in the air then seemed to lean forward. They were on their way.

He didn't ask where. Judging by their bruised conditions and where they'd been, he knew the first stop would be the hospital.

Tilting his head back, he sighed and closed his eyes. That had been a close one. Too close. SAC Mitchell wouldn't be pleased to hear about his demolished SUV. Between him and Jack Quinn, they'd destroyed two in the line of duty in the past few years. Neither time had been their fault, of course. Just par for the course when one worked with the FBI. He huffed out a soft chuckle and opened his eyes. His glance met Fran's. An adorable pucker formed in the center of her forehead and the corners of her lips curled down. Her warm amber gaze scanned him. He felt that look to the depth of his being and instinctively sat up, holding in a groan when his side protested.

She'd been worried for him.

Tanner rubbed his chest without thinking about it. He wasn't used to people worrying about him or fretting over his well-being. Well, no one except his mom. But that was kind of in her job description.

His brothers, sisters, and even his dad accepted his risks as part of his life as an FBI special agent. And, he admitted to himself, he often downplayed the dangers he'd waded into while working a case. The fact that most of his work was classified and couldn't be shared with civilians made this easier.

Francesca Brown was a different story. She knew first-hand the dangers involved in working with law enforcement of any branch. Whether it was local or federal. While he could get away with giving his family nonchalant answers and glossing over the real horrors he sometimes faced in his work, he couldn't do that with her. Because she faced some of the same challenges.

And today her life had been put in danger in the worst way. And still she managed to care for others.

When Sean had first introduced his wife, Tanner had acknowledged to himself that she was lovely. Then Sean had been killed and Tanner had added a new layer to what he knew about Fran. She was brave and exuded strength, even while her world imploded.

Now, gazing at her, awe sparked to life inside his chest. Despite everything, he admired her compassion and her ability to deal with the unthinkable while bullets flew about them. Such as the way she'd selflessly protected the little boy with her own body while they'd gone over the edge.

There were days when he worried that he had forgotten how to be compassionate, times when he worried that he was losing his humanity because he faced so much evil.

Not her. She was as strong and steady as they came, and had still managed to hold that small child in a maternal embrace.

A sudden desire to be worthy of such a woman rose in his soul. He squashed it down. Amazing, she might be. And no one could argue that Francesca Brown was gorgeous and graceful.

Tanner ripped his gaze from hers. She might be all that. A few years ago, he would have pursued her. That was before a car bomb nearly took him out, shredding his shoulder, back and the side of his neck in the process, leaving permanent scars. Tanner didn't consider himself a vain man. He hadn't thought the damage would be much of an issue, but the woman he'd been involved with at the time had let him know in very clear terms that she found it embarrassing when he wore a shirt that allowed the scars on his neck to show. People tended to stare and point. Tanner had shrugged off the attention, but she hadn't been able to take that kind of reaction. He'd been ready to go shopping for a ring. Her rejection had cut deeply.

He wouldn't put himself through that again. Especially since he had no desire to leave the FBI, which meant he'd possibly end up in a similar situation at some future point in his career.

He could never let himself fall for Fran. But he would find the person out to get her.

And hopefully learn who had killed Sean in the process.

Fran hadn't been this exhausted since after Sean had died. Every muscle ached. She didn't dare look at herself, knowing she'd see a walking bruise with black hair wearing faded jeans and sparkly rubber boots. She grimaced. This was not the image she cared to portray to the outside world.

But it couldn't be helped. And she knew appearances masked a wealth of pain and secrets, some beautiful, and some devastating or even hideous. Her own family had proved that.

Tanner muffled another groan. It didn't matter how stoically he sat in the helicopter, the white line circling his lips, which were pressed tightly together, told a story of its own. He was in agony and trying to disguise it. She'd seen it in his eyes before he'd torn them away from hers.

The helicopter surged through the air toward the hospital. She swayed slightly on her seat. Every time it struck turbulence, Tanner's hands flexed and clenched on the edge of his bench. Was he in pain? Somehow, she got the feeling there was more than physical discomfort at play. Fran winced in sympathy, keeping her thoughts to herself. She hated letting people see her when her emotions were raw. Turning her gaze away, she allowed him his privacy.

They'd soon arrive and be treated. Then maybe she could get some answers.

The little boy in her arms lay still. Looking down at him, she didn't know if she should be relieved or worried that he seemed to have fallen asleep again. What kind of trauma had he endured? Hopefully, he was just too exhausted to handle the stress. Her eyes slid over his face and what she could see of his body. No visible wounds or blood. He didn't seem to be in pain. But some children had a high pain tolerance.

Instinctively, she tightened her arms around him. Even in his sleep, he flinched. She loosened her grip. She wouldn't push for more than he could handle. Instead, she'd count herself fortunate that he seemed to tolerate her closeness.

Sighing, she faced the window and stared at the scenery flashing by.

Many people had misconceptions about autism. She knew from her niece that relationships presented a challenge. Things most people took for granted, such as making eye contact or answering questions, were difficult, and for some impossible. Loud noises or too much happening in the environment tended to be overstimulating and would send Lucy into a tantrum.

Had any of that changed in the past five years? Suddenly, she ached to talk with her sister Anastasia and know they were doing well. It had hurt when her parents had cut her out of their lives, but their relationship had been contentious for years. Sometimes, not having to argue daily about her choices seemed like a relief. When Stacy had severed ties with her, Fran had been gutted.

Would she ever see her sister again, or was her entire family lost forever?

The unbearable idea made her shudder. She'd been three when Stacy had been born. Although separated by several years, they'd been close growing up. Fran had always been protective of her sister when their parents had come down too hard on her, such as when she'd wanted to take a creative writing class in high school. That was not acceptable. Reading was good, as long as the books were appropriate, but writing was too bohemian for their family.

No daughter of mine will go into any field related to the arts, their father had yelled.

It wouldn't have mattered what field Fran had planned on going into. She had always been the daughter who'd rebelled, the one who'd wanted more than to find a wealthy husband and join the country club set. Her family equated success with tangible possessions and diplomas on the wall from private schools and Ivy League colleges.

Fran had had zero interest in fitting into that mold. Instead of wealth, she'd craved knowledge. For as long as she could recall, her every thought and move had been dissected and criticized. Even though Stacy had been several years younger, her parents, especially her mother, had harped constantly about what a perfect daughter Anastasia was and how Francesca would do well to follow her lead.

The break, when it happened, had been discouraging, but not unexpected.

The helicopter dipped. Her stomach plunged, shaking her out of her reverie.

"No, no, no, no." The child in her arms started chanting, his agitated words rising.

If she didn't distract him, it would soon become a shriek. Grabbing the ends of Tanner's jacket, she wrapped the little boy up snuggly, like a little taco. He settled almost immediately, his yells giving way to the horrible but softer sound of grinding teeth.

"How do you know what to do?"

She glanced up into Tanner's pale face. "My niece, Lucy, did what is called self-stimming when she became agitated."

"Stimming?"

She nodded. "Stimulating. When a child with sensory integration issues is frustrated or anxious, they have a set of repetitive gestures or actions that can create the stimulation they need to calm themselves. Such as the grinding of the teeth. Or rocking."

"I can't even imagine. I hope we can locate the little guy's family."

She frowned. "I do too. Do you think it will prove to be a problem?"

He shrugged then sucked in a breath. "Ugh. Forgot about my ribs. I don't know. Jared was no longer in Ohio. He'd been hiding in Indiana. Which makes me question why he'd come back to Indiana and where was he when he picked this kiddo up."

"As soon as we get to the station, I'll ask Chief Spencer for some space to check the database for missing Amish children in Ohio, Pennsylvania and Indiana."

"There might not be a report," he warned her. "If the family hasn't notified the authorities, which is very possible, then we're right back where we started. Nowhere."

"I'll worry about that if it happens. Maybe you can use Officer Meek's station. He's out for the week following a minor surgery."

"Oh yeah? I hadn't heard Joe—"

The child jerked his head. "Joey. Joey." He continued to repeat the name, his voice sounding almost happy for the first time.

"Is that his name?" she asked. Leaning away to look into his face, she cautiously said, "Joey?"

In response, he glanced up and patted her face, almost but not quite meeting her eyes.

"I guess it is. Why won't he make eye contact? Do you think he has a vision loss too?"

Any answer she might have made was swallowed up when the chopper jolted. Glancing at the ground below, she saw the hospital landing pad, looking like a round yawning mouth ready to devour them. Shuddering, she turned her head from the sight. She had way too much imagination.

The child in her arms began chanting.

"One star, two star, three star."

He was counting the stars printed on her shirt again. She'd definitely need to locate more patterned blouses.

"I think he's calming himself by counting," Tanner observed.

She blinked. He'd picked up on the boy's motivation pretty quickly for someone unused to being around children with autism.

The helicopter settled onto the pad. A stream of people equipped with stretchers poured from the building. Tanner scowled but awkwardly allowed himself to be loaded onto one of the stretchers.

"Get Fran and the kid first," he demanded.

Joey, hopefully that was really his name, wanted nothing to do with that plan. He screamed and clung onto Fran, his little hands gripping like iron clamps and digging into her arms.

"I don't think he'll let me put him down," she told the orderly. "I'm not injured."

"Policy, ma'am."

"Fine." She didn't mean to snap, but she had used her daily quota of patience. "If I could sit in a wheelchair, I'll hold him in my lap."

After they all were settled, the orderly began to move the wheelchair forward.

"Dr. Spelling, call on line two."

The sound of the PA system calling for some unknown physician turned her blood to ice.

Fran had been so distracted by Joey, she'd forgotten one very important fact.

They were at the hospital. The one place on earth that sent her into panic attacks. She couldn't afford to have one now.

FIVE

When she'd first taken the job as a forensic artist, visiting hospitals had been a routine part of the work. She hated seeing people suffer, but it was one of the duties she'd had to accept to make the drawings and catch the criminals or find the missing persons.

Six years ago, that had changed with one phone call. Now going to the hospital caused panic to fill her veins.

Usually, she took a few minutes to mentally prepare herself before entering the dreaded facility. Today, she didn't have that luxury. The moment the emergency doors slid open, a deluge of memories flooded her brain, drowning her, blocking out the chaos surrounding her. Her arms tightened convulsively around Joey. Squeezing her eyes shut, she could still hear the phone ringing, and the sound of Kathy's voice informing her that Sean had been injured and was being rushed to the hospital.

Fran practically had the detailing from the steering wheel imprinted on the palms of her hands because she'd held it so tightly as she'd driven to the hospital. Even though it had been a clear day outside, she'd felt as though she'd been moving through a thunderstorm. Tears had clouded her vision. Her sleeves became soaked from constantly wiping her face.

She'd made it to the hospital and hadn't even bothered parking her car or grabbing her keys. She'd left it running under the main entrance awning. Grabbing her purse, she had dashed inside, hitting the reception counter hard enough to leave bruises on her stomach. She hadn't felt it at the time.

Fortunately, the people at the hospital had been kind. They'd known her because of her job and they'd been expecting her. A veteran nurse known for her stern nature had gently caught her by the elbow and ushered her into the emergency room.

The memory of her first glimpse of her husband lying on a gurney haunted her. Dried blood coated his face and neck. It was everywhere. For a moment, she had barely recognized him. When she gasped, he'd opened his lids and murmured her name. More droplets had gurgled from his mouth and dribbled down his chin. At that moment, she'd understood he wouldn't survive.

Fran had been wearing her favorite white silk blouse. She'd been in court and had wanted to look her best. Since the day she'd purchased that blouse, she had taken particular care with it. Seeing Sean in pain, it had no longer mattered. Nothing had mattered except the man lying before her, his life seeping out of him from internal wounds while the doctors and nurses had stood by, helpless. She'd gathered her husband to her, regardless of the blood covering her arms and clothes. No one had stopped her or demanded she be careful, confirming what she'd already known.

A shriek in her ear wrenched her away from the past.

Joey squirmed in her lap.

"Sorry, buddy. I didn't mean to hold you so tight." She rubbed his back in a steady circular motion. He calmed after a few seconds and relaxed against her, his gaze avoiding the ceiling. "Is there a way I can get a newspaper or something to shade his eyes from the overhead lights?"

She didn't know who grabbed it, but within seconds someone thrust a newspaper into her grasp. She held it above his head.

"Hold on."

The paramedics steered Tanner into a cubicle, closing the curtain behind him.

Fran's heart sped up. She was alone in the emergency room with this child.

She pushed her fear down. Joey needed her to remain calm. She was his anchor right now, the one person he knew and depended on. When he started counting the stars on her shirt again, she counted along with him.

As the orderly began to move them into a cubicle, she asked him to wait. "This child, he's in police custody and he has autism. The sounds and bright lights are disturbing. Is there a way we can bring him into an office, or another room, to be examined? Somewhere that there isn't so much stimulation or light?"

The man frowned. When he opened his mouth, another voice spoke over his.

"I'm Dr. Blair. You can use my office. This way." The tall physician strode away without checking to see if they were following. When someone called to him, he switched directions. "I'll be in the moment I'm free."

The orderly muttered something under his breath, but obeyed and pushed the wheelchair along. By this time, Fran's arm began to ache. Experimentally, she dropped the arm holding the newspaper an inch or two. Joey started shaking his head against her chest. She cautiously switched arms so she wouldn't jostle him. He settled. When the child shivered and shoved his face into her shoulder, she lifted the coat to gently cover his head. "I think the light bothers him."

The orderly shrugged and wheeled her into an office. Shutting the door, he dimmed one of the lights. "The doctor will be in soon."

It was a relief to drop the newspaper. She knew soon could be two hours later. Where was Tanner? How would they figure this out? It felt overwhelming, dealing with the case of Jared's and her husband's murders, while being hunted with an unidentified Amish child.

She'd been in tough situations before, but this time she had no control over the outcome. They were sitting ducks, waiting for someone to find them and shoot them down.

And she had no idea why.

It was nearly an hour later when the doctor returned. By the time she and Joey had been examined and declared fit to be released, Joey had reached his limit. Tanner's jacket had been abandoned during the evaluation. Fran grabbed it and wrapped it around the child, humming soothingly in his ear. Between the pressure of the jacket swaddling him and the monotone noise, his rocking slowed and his agitated outbursts ceased.

"You're good at that," Dr. Blair commented. He picked up a large Koosh ball off the desk and handed it to Joey. The child was fascinated with it, running his hands over the textured toy. "Have you contacted Children and Youth about him?"

Fran froze. "No."

"If you want, I can do that."

"That won't be necessary, Doctor." Tanner entered the room, his stride rather stiff. "We'll take care of whatever needs to be done."

"Did they bandage your ribs?" She frowned at him. Broken bones were always painful.

He shook his head. "No need. I don't know how it's possible, but nothing's broken. My entire stomach and chest, however, is one continuous bruise, so I'll be feeling the effects of that airbag for a few days."

"How are we getting to the station?" She gently stood Joey beside her, praying he wouldn't react. He remained absorbed in the toy. She hoped Dr. Blair wasn't expecting her to hand it back to him. Ripping the ball from Joey's hands would instantly decimate the layer of trust that had started to develop between them. Once gone, it would be impossible to reestablish without lots of time and effort.

While she didn't mind expending the effort to help a child, any child, time was not something they had in spades.

"We can buy you a new ball," she informed the doctor, hoping he wouldn't object.

He waved her words aside. "Don't worry about it. He needs it more than I do."

She couldn't argue with that.

Tanner tapped her shoulder. She turned to him, startled at the jolt of electricity at his touch. She shrugged his hand away. "You shocked me."

He looked a bit surprised himself, but quickly recovered. "Sorry. Lieutenant Bartlett is waiting outside to give us a ride."

"Kathy's here? Great. We can start looking for this guy's family."

She reached out and gently took Joey's hand in hers. "Joey. We're going now."

To her surprise, Joey went without fuss.

Kathy waited right outside the building, parked just beyond the awning that covered the entrance. She saw them coming and stepped out of the police cruiser.

"Hey. I grabbed a booster seat on my way here."

Fran bit her lip.

"What?" Kathy propped her fists on her trim hips and glared at her friend. "What did I miss?"

"Nothing. A booster seat was an entirely appropriate thing to grab. Except, he's Amish. I'm not sure if he'll sit in it."

"For that matter," Tanner added, "will he let us put the seat belt on him?"

She sighed. "Only one way to find out. Tanner, you better ride in front with Kathy."

It would have been easier to put a greased pig in a harness than it was to strap Joey into the booster seat. But safety rules were in place for a reason, so she persevered until he was sitting in the seat, clutching the ball and counting the individual threads. Sweat trickled down the back of her neck and was absorbed by her cotton shirt.

Ugh. She felt grimy, tired, and hungry.

"All set?" Kathy asked.

"Just go." Fran closed her eyes briefly, breathing a quiet prayer for patience and grace. She remained in that attitude for an extra moment, soaking in the blessed silence.

"Kathy, look out!" Tanner bellowed.

Fran's eyes popped open. Her head swiveled on her neck to locate the danger.

She found it in the form of a large green pickup bearing down on them.

Kathy jerked the steering wheel to evade the truck. "Someone needs a ticket or two," she growled.

"He's turning around," Tanner announced, his voice grim.

Fran craned her neck and peered out the back window.

Sure enough, the truck did a U-turn smack in the middle of Main Street, cutting off several cars. Horns blared. The pickup kept coming.

"He's got a gun!" she said a moment before the first shot rang out. It missed.

"We have to lead him away from the civilians before we engage," Tanner said.

The police vehicle surged forward. Fran trembled. They couldn't keep going at this speed. There was too much traffic. They were going to hit someone.

She'd seriously underestimated her friend. Kathy swung the wheel wide, sending the cruiser toward the grass. It crashed into the curb and went over it. Fran felt the jolt all the way to her bones. Kathy continued across the grass, cutting a wide swath around the cars on the road. The truck roared up behind them. When Kathy turned off the grass and onto a back road, the shooter followed.

A second shot rang out. Fran heard it thunk into the cruiser. They'd probably find the bullet in the trunk. He might have had a gun, but so did Kathy and Tanner. They were out of the traffic and there were no people in view.

"Open my window," Tanner said.

Kathy did as he requested. He unbuckled his seat belt and slid out the window until he was sitting on the sill, his SIG Sauer in his hands. Fran held her breath. If he fell...

She blocked the thought. Tanner knew what he was doing.

Keeping quiet so she wouldn't distract them, she kept praying for rescue as Tanner took aim. He might not get another shot.

"Keep it steady, Kathy!" Tanner yelled.

He had the truck in his sights. He didn't want to hurt

anyone. If he could take out a tire, slow the pickup down so he'd have a chance to slap handcuffs on them and throw them in a cell… How were these guys connected to Jared and Joey?

Narrowing his gaze, he squeezed the trigger. His bullet slammed into the front tire. The truck's engine revved. Instead of slowing, the driver shifted gears and sped backward. At the intersection, the green pickup took off without stopping, clipping several cars in its path. More horns and cursing followed.

There was no way they'd catch it.

"I got the make and model," Fran stated.

Tanner raised an eyebrow at her.

"What? When you work with the police, you pick up a few things."

"I'm not complaining." Tanner settled back into his seat. Kathy was already on the radio, calling the incident in. They'd have to interview all the people whose vehicles had been hit by the fleeing truck. It was going to be a long night.

"Too bad we didn't get a license plate," Fran muttered. Not all cars in Ohio had front and back plates. By the time the truck had turned around, it had been too far away for her to read the plates.

Joey began to chant to himself.

"We can't leave until someone else comes to relieve me," Kathy said. "I'm first on the scene."

Tanner rolled his window back up. He twisted around so he sat eye to eye with Fran. Her calm amber gaze fused with his, soothing him. His glance transferred to Joey. The Amish child remained in his seat, his attention focused inward. He continued muttering random numbers to himself. He seemed uninjured.

"I know a bullet struck the car. Were either of you hurt?"

Fran shook her head, her full lips tilting up at the corners in the barest hint of a smile. He blinked, unnerved by how that subtle shift in her expression caused his stomach to flip.

"We're fine. I think it hit the trunk."

When Kathy parked the car in a store parking lot and got out of the vehicle, Tanner hesitated. "I should go and help her, at least for a few minutes. Are you two safe here?"

Fran nodded. "We'll be fine. Just don't go too far."

He locked the car and left. When Kathy saw him, she waved him over.

"Agent Hall, can you do traffic control?"

It wasn't his favorite duty, but he readily agreed, knowing someone had to take it on. He maneuvered himself so he had a clear view of the police cruiser at all times. He'd been at it for maybe thirty minutes when their relief showed up. Two cops exited their patrol car. Kathy waved the younger one over.

"Take my cruiser back to the station. I need to stay here."

The cop gulped. He must have been a rookie. "I can't take your car! What—"

Her mouth flattened in a straight line. "Look, there's a young boy inside my car. He has autism. It was hard getting him in my car. If we try and transfer him, it might really traumatize him. I'll catch a ride with Officer McCoy when we're done here."

"Do you need me to stay, Lieutenant?"

"Thanks for the offer, Special Agent Hall. I appreciate it. But I think you should stick with Fran and the kid."

He didn't argue. When he stepped into the vehicle, the first thing he noted was that Joey was still chanting the same numbers over and over. Tanner settled back in his seat and took his phone out. He didn't have his computer, but he could make notes on his phone and sync them. Writing down the events of the day helped clarify things in his mind. He also wrote several questions he needed the answers to. Such as, what happened to Jared? Why was Jared at Sean's old house?

That was the one that really puzzled him. Jared and Sean had worked closely together, but Sean had been dead for years. Jared knew this. Nor had the young man ever met Fran. He could see no reason for the detour.

At the station, Tanner put his phone away and assisted Fran and Joey from the car. Joey barely seemed to notice them. He allowed himself to be corralled into the building and into the conference room. Kathy had called ahead. The chief had food waiting for them. Joey saw the chicken nuggets and French fries and immediately ran to the table and grabbed a handful of food. He scooted himself into a corner and ate his fast-food dinner.

Fran and Tanner sat at the table.

"I thought we'd have a fight on our hands to get him in here," he confessed.

She frowned, her gaze moving to the child before returning to Tanner. "I did, too, but he keeps saying the same sequence of letters and numbers over and over. It's not a phone number, and I'm sure it's not random. Because they are the same."

For the moment, the child was focused on his food.

Suddenly, Fran sat up straight. "Tanner! The sequence! We'd been talking about a license plate. What if he is reciting a license plate number?"

They turned in tandem and stared at Joey. He walked over to Fran and put his hand on her face, but still wouldn't meet her gaze. Tanner was stunned at the level of connectedness Joey displayed toward the attractive brunette.

"What is it, Joey? Is that a license plate number?" Fran's gentle voice tugged at his heart.

The boy gave a dreamy smile and repeated the sequence again. And again.

Tanner hooked up to the FBI's Vehicle File on the National Crime Information Center. The NCIC was a database that kept track of information related to criminal activity. When that search revealed nothing useful, he switched to the motor vehicle registration in Ohio.

"We've got a hit!" he crowed. If this panned out, they might have answers before the day ended. He looked closer at the information and his elation faded. The vehicle listed was not the truck they'd been chased by.

"What's wrong?"

Distracted, he leaned back in his chair, pushing his feet against the floor until the front legs lifted off the ground and the chair was balancing on two legs. He kept one hand on the table to anchor himself.

"Tanner! You're going to tip that chair clear over and hurt yourself," Fran snapped.

He raised his feet. The chair crashed back to its original position. "Sorry. It's kind of a bad habit when I'm thinking."

"That's great. But can you let me in on what you're thinking about?" A bit of the snippiness leaked from her tone. She sounded more amused than annoyed now. Casting a quick cast across the table at her, he grimaced. Her expression greatly reminded him of the one his mom had worn just before she'd compared Tanner and his brothers to a group of children.

He ignored her smirk and waved his hand at the computer screen. "This license plate. It's registered to Darcy Humes."

"And?" Her eyebrows rose in a question.

"So that's an alias." He tapped out a name in the database. When the driver's license photo popped up on his computer screen, he spun the device around, allowing her to view the image. She gasped in recognition.

"That's—"

"Yep. Darcy Murray. Wife of convicted felon Judge George Murray."

Now they needed to figure out why Joey was reciting the plate number of a woman who'd disappeared months ago and if it had anything to do with the death of her son.

"Darcy. Darcy," Joey chanted. "Darcy go away."

Fran swallowed. There were several ways to take Joey's words. Either the woman had left, was taken away, or she'd died. Which was it? The perpetual knot in her stomach seemed to grow several inches.

"Obviously, he knew her," Tanner whispered. "I've got a slew of questions, but the first one is where did he last see her and the car. If we could find Darcy, or at least where she was with him, maybe we can finally gather some clues as to who he is and what happened to Jared and his mother."

"I don't think it can be good."

"I agree, but we have to know."

Fran chewed on her bottom lip, wincing when she bit a little too hard. Next to her, Joey carried on a conversation with himself, although she could only make out every five or six words because the majority of it was in Pennsylvania Dutch.   Over the past few years, she'd befriended several Amish residents of Sutter Springs, particular the Bender family, who she knew through Joss Beck, Sergeant Steve Beck's wife and the daughter of Nathan and Edith Bender. Her Amish friends were very fluent in English and spoke it without fail when in her presence, or when they were talking with non-Amish neighbors. However, she knew it was their second language. They spoke in their own language in their homes. Once they began attending the Amish school, the children were expected to speak English while there. Had Joey started school yet? He didn't look old enough, but he might be older than he appeared.

Joey seemed to be either retelling something that had happened or creating a scenario in his brain. Whichever it was, he was content.

"What do we do about him?" She pitched her voice low. "The hospital wanted to know if we had contacted social services. I can't imagine leaving him with just anyone. Not after the trauma he's been through."

Tanner gave her a tender smile. She blinked. Normally, his smiles were impersonal, or mischievous. But this expression made her breath catch in her throat. She preferred the other smiles. They didn't cause complicated feelings to rise in her soul.

"You've bonded a little with him. It's understandable. But he's not going anywhere yet."

"Oh? Why is that?"

"Because I talked with Chief Spencer while you were busy with him. The chief agrees with me that, right now, Joey is in danger. He needs to have more protection than he'd get at someone's house. Plus, if we placed him with a family, we would put the family and other foster children in danger."

"Added to that," the chief commented as he entered the room, "this child has some keen observation skills. I don't know what else is stored in his mind, but he might be the key to breaking several cold cases wide open. I believe, since you've developed some rapport with him, Fran, that it would be beneficial if you were involved in his case."

She didn't like it. Not that she minded helping. She

didn't. "He can't stay at my house, Chief. It's not child-proofed. And it's a bit out of the way. If something happened there, it might take too long for help to arrive."

"I am still working out the details about where you'll stay, or what to do with him at night. I can't keep a little one at the police station. Give me some time. I'll figure something out."

She wasn't about to tell the chief of police no.

"We need to find the vehicle that fired shots at us, and hopefully whoever was driving it," Tanner said.

Fran nodded. Idly she plucked a pencil and one of the white legal pads the chief kept in the conference room from the center of the table and began to doodle. Sometimes it helped her think. After a moment, she realized Joey's attention was riveted on the pad. On a hunch, she set it on the table in front of him. She drew a quick sketch of Tanner and pointed first to the man then to his image on the paper.

Joey followed her finger. "Tanner."

"That's right." Encouraged, she pulled Tanner's computer around again and pointed to the picture of Darcy.

"Where is Darcy, Joey?"

She didn't expect an answer. He was, after all, only four or five. Six at the most.

Joey grabbed the pad and pencil and drew a perfect picture of Darcy, her face contorted in fear. He then drew a building. The building itself wasn't very clearly drawn. What was clear were the numbers on the front of it.

"Tanner. I think this may be the address, maybe where he was kept. Or where he met Darcy."

"Maybe it's his house?"

She shook her head. "No. Amish homes are all white. I remember Joss Beck saying it was so they were all alike and no one stood out. Even when an Amish family moves into a house, they have one year to paint it white and remove the electricity. It's an important element of the Amish belief system. This looks like a brick house. I don't think an Amish family would ever buy a house like that."

"Hmm. Things would be simpler if we had a street name, but I can work with this." Tanner grunted, his gaze never lifting from the screen. He began plunking keys on the keyboard. "With today's technology, you can locate anything with a house number."

She held her breath, watching his forehead wrinkle as his brows furrowed, his blue eyes narrowed behind his wire-rimmed glasses. Then she noticed the way he typed, one finger at a time. Stifling a snicker, she brushed her hand across her lips to hide her amusement. It was rather endearing.

He grabbed a second tablet and scribbled down an address. Then another. With every address he wrote, her heart sank a little more. That was a lot of houses with the same number. He circled several of the addresses and looked up. She straightened in her chair.

"We have lots of possible addresses, but there are six a reasonable distance from here."

She grimaced. "Will we have to drive to all six?"

She dreaded the thought of wasting time when a killer was two steps behind them.

Tanner scoffed, the slightest sneer curling the edge of his nostrils. "Of course not. We'll look them up and see if we can see the houses from a street view. Then we'll show them to Joey. And if he doesn't react, we'll show him the others I found until he responds. He's bound to react to one of them."

She bit her lip. She didn't want to burst his bubble. But… "What if the address isn't in Ohio? It could be in Indiana.

You said something about Jared going to Indiana. Or it might be Pennsylvania. You know there are Amish communities spread all over the country. There's even one in Texas."

"You're kidding."

"Serious."

"Well, if it's not one of these on the list, then we'll expand our search."

He fiddled around on the keyboard for another twenty seconds or so, then swiveled the device around to give them a view of the first house. It was odd knowing that technology gave one the ability to view a house, any house, up close. The first image had a woman sweeping the front porch. It seemed rather invasive.

"It would be great if we got an image of a person in the house. Especially if it were the killer. Or would give us a clue."

He nodded, but kept his attention riveted on Joey. The child glanced at the screen then looked away. His expression never changed. "I'm going to go out on a limb and say this isn't the house."

He pulled the computer back toward himself and typed in the second address.

"The nice thing is, this will take a lot of the leg work out," she mused. "Save us some time."

"Yeah. Okay, this house isn't brick, so I'm going to say it's not the one we want. This one is half brick. Maybe…"

He shoved the laptop back toward them. Again, Joey showed zero interest.

"Third time's the charm, right?" He found another address and repeated the process. "This house is out of the Sutter Springs jurisdiction, though."

Joey glanced at the screen then reacted as if he'd been electrified. He lifted his feet onto the chair, wrapped his arms around his knees and dropped his head onto them. He began to rock back and forth, humming loudly.

They'd found the house.

Hopefully, they'd find someone alive when they arrived.

Tanner couldn't remember the last time he'd felt this helpless. Joey sat less than two feet away in abject misery, and for the life of him, Tanner could not think of a single way to lesson his distress. Was it all fear? Or was some of it sadness?

Who knew what kind of trauma the child had experienced. He recalled the way Joey had rocked and cried when they'd found him in the yard.

Fran, amazing woman that she was, began drawing birds on her pad, counting them as she sketched them. He'd never seen anyone draw anything so fast. They were so realistic, they looked like they could take flight from her sketchpad. Joey stopped humming. His rocking slowed.

When she reached six, he tilted his head so one eye peeked over at the birds on the paper. By the time she drew the eighth bird, he let his legs fall over the edge of the seat and counted with her. He pointed to the first bird. *"Vogel."*

"That must be how he'd say it in Pennsylvania Dutch. *Vogel*," she repeated. "Bird."

He didn't echo the English word. But Tanner was sure she was correct. She seemed to understand Joey on a deeper level.

Averting his eyes from them, he zeroed in on the picture of the house on his laptop that had sent Joey into a tailspin.

What was that in the window? Narrowing his eyes, Tanner stared at the hazy image. Near the edge of the glass, he could make out a pale shape with some darker coloration, but nothing distinct. Whatever or whoever it was, it was almost completely clear of the window. If it was a person, it might have been a deliberate decision. Or not.

Of course, this image may have been captured long before any nefarious deeds had happened on the premises.

Enlarging the scene as much as the laptop would allow did no good. While the image grew larger, it also blurred. He shrank it down again. Maybe he could take a picture of that one part and enlarge it? Leaning over slightly, he grabbed the phone from his front pocket and snapped a photo, then used his thumb and forefinger to zoom in.

There. What was a barely visible item before, now appeared to be a biceps. Male, he'd say, judging by the muscles and the cut of the sleeve. However, not conclusive since that was the only portion of the arm visible. There was a tattoo of some kind on the arm, but no matter how hard he tried, or how focused he aimed, the image remained vague.

Wordlessly, he beckoned Fran closer. When she leaned in, he aimed the tablet toward her and pointed out the tattoo. Her mouth formed a silent "O."

The door of the conference swung inward. Chief Spencer strode into the room. He was a soft-spoken man, but there was no denying the air of authority he wore like a second skin. He was a man who relished being in charge. Tanner had worked with him once before. He'd rapidly developed a healthy respect for Chief Spencer's instincts and the way he took care of those under his command.

"Agent Hall. Fran."

Fran sat back in her seat. Her brow puckered. Every second she stared at the chief, the deeper the lines became. "Whatever you have to say, I'm not going to like it, am I?"

Tanner blinked. He thought he'd started to understand how she thought. She was poised. Polished. Since meeting her again, he was seeing a new side to her. Slightly snarky. Still sweet, but with a little bite to her.

Realizing he was gaping, Tanner yanked his attention from her.

"You probably won't like it," the chief agreed. "I've called social services."

"But I thought—"

He held up a hand, halting her arguments. "I know we can't place him with a family. It's too dangerous. I've arranged for him to stay with a social worker under guard at a hotel."

If her frown became any fiercer, those lines would be permanent. "I understand, sir. But he's bonded with me. I really feel I should be with him until we find his family. And you said I needed to remain part of this case."

He was already shaking his head. "You are part of this case. I do want you working with him. But as far as you providing his protective detail? No can do. I want you available if we need you. This case involving the son of Judge Murray is a serious matter. As is the possibility that the judge's wife might be out there. If there's a living witness that can give us a description of whoever shot at you and Agent Hall, or those who kidnapped this little guy, I don't want you to be hindered in any way. This case is your priority. Otherwise, we might never find his family."

She ducked her head, but not before Tanner witnessed her scowl.

"Besides, you can't carry a gun while on duty. You know that. If someone attacked you or him, how would you protect him? Or yourself?" When she didn't argue, the chief swiveled his focus to Tanner. "Have we learned anything new?"

"Yes, sir." Tanner updated him on the house they'd located based on Joey's drawing and his reaction. He also mentioned the tattooed arm he'd seen in the window. "I don't know if it's relevant, but it might be."

The chief tilted his head. "I believe this qualifies for exigent circumstances. From what you've told me, you have probable cause to believe one or more people are in immediate danger. Go now. I'll send some officers with you. We need to search the house tonight."

Tanner agreed and rose to his feet. Fran still wasn't happy, but she stood as well. The fate of Darcy Murray was on all their minds. What were the chances they'd find her alive?

Only to himself, he admitted he held out little hope for her.

The chief called a team together and had Tanner brief them on where they were going and what they hoped to find. "Special Agent Hall will be in authority for our team. You'll be out of our jurisdiction. This touches on a federal case, though. I've contacted the local police department. They'll be standing by. Don't step on any toes. This is their precinct."

A soft murmur of agreement ran through the room. Some of them might not like it, but they were professionals and would abide by Chief Spencer's rules. It was a good thing. Sometimes, Tanner got a little pushback from cops who felt he was digging around in their cases, messing with their territory.

"Agent Hall," a young officer called out, half raising his hand as if he were school. "It's nearly five o'clock. By the time we arrive, it will be seven."

He nodded. "Yeah. It will be touch and go. We won't have more than an hour or so of daylight. Hopefully, we'll find what we need inside."

Ten minutes later, they were ready to ride.

"Fran, why don't you ride with me?" Kathy Bartlett asked.

"You, too, Tanner. I hear you don't have a replacement car yet."

It wasn't a question. He grimaced. He'd hear the sound of that black SUV crashing down out of the tree in his nightmares. It had been a harrowing experience. But no one had died, so he'd chalk it up as a win.

"Yeah, no. No replacement yet. I appreciate the ride."

"Fran?"

She nodded, her expression distracted. Tanner noted she'd located another sketch pad. It made sense that she'd keep a spare tucked at the police station if she spent any amount of time here. He waved her ahead of him. She seemed fragile, which he knew she wasn't. The urge to place a protective hand on her shoulder startled him. That would definitely not be cool. Or welcome. But she worried him. Every ten seconds or so, her gaze slid toward the conference room.

Clearly, her thoughts were all wrapped up in Joey.

He had to admit, he wasn't keen on leaving the boy with strangers. Not after seeing how well he'd taken to Francesca. But it wasn't his call. A keening wail rose from the conference room. He winced and looked down at Fran. She'd paled.

"Francesca?"

She lifted her face to meet his gaze. Despite the anguish shining like a beacon from her amber eyes, she mashed her lips together and straightened her shoulders. No. Not fragile. Strength radiated from her. She'd borne much, and would handle much more, to get the job done.

His admiration for her grew. He nodded at her and let her walk out the door first. They had work to do.

What he needed to do was to find the person or people involved and get to the bottom of this case. He wouldn't rest until Joey and Francesca were safe.

SIX

She'd come close to losing control back at the station.

Too close.

Fran had built a reputation for herself since Sean's passing. His death, or his murder, had completely shattered her. Never again. She should have known she couldn't have happiness. Not after her parents and sister had rejected her, and then the loss of the baby she'd already grown to cherish. She prided herself on always being professional and in complete charge of her emotions. She'd once heard a couple of cops at another police department refer to her as "ice cold."

She didn't care. Not about making friends, or being beloved by all. She was in her line of work because she loved forensics and the ability to help close a case. Her favorite cases were those where she helped reunite families. Such as she wanted to do for Joey.

Don't go there, she warned herself. That little boy had wrapped himself around her heart so fast, she'd been ready to argue with the chief when he'd informed her of the plans he'd made. That's when she'd known she'd gotten too close.

She needed distance. At least she still had her faith. She'd been angry at God but had never doubted His presence in her life.

She paid no attention to the conversation between Tanner and Kathy until Kathy bumped into a curb while parallel parking in front of the house. What? Kathy never bounced off the curbs. She saw the other woman watching her in the mirror. Oh. It was for her benefit. Kathy, her best friend, was giving her a heads-up, giving her time to put her game face on before they met the local police department.

Being in the back of a police cruiser was a new experience for Fran. When she tried to open the door from the inside, it wouldn't budge. She huffed and waited for Tanner to open the door for her.

The local police team stood in a group on the sidewalk. They had a K-9 and handler with them. The dog was a gorgeous German shepherd outfitted in an army-green harness. The dog's handler held the lead in her hands.

Tanner and Kathy were standing next to a tall, muscular man, talking. He was obviously the one in charge on this end.

He nodded and held up his hands. "Listen up, people." He spoke softly so his voice wouldn't carry beyond the group of law enforcement surrounding him. Neighbors were streaming from the houses up and down the block to watch. "This is Special Agent Hall and Lieutenant Bartlett from Sutter Springs. They received credible intel that a crime might have been committed here, or might still be happening. Lives are at stake. What we know is that no one has been seen coming in or out of this house in three days, as far as the neighbors can tell."

So, they'd already canvassed the neighborhood. That would save them some time.

"We are acting on the assumption there is an active threat inside the house."

A nearly tangible wave swept through the group of law

enforcement personnel. Tanner removed his jacket. She hadn't even noticed the Kevlar vest he'd put on under it before they'd left the station. A flurry of weapons leaving their holsters surrounded her. Except for the dog, she was the only one in the company who was unarmed.

Kathy slid through the crowd to stand next to her. "Fran, do you think you should wait in the car?"

"No." She injected as much attitude into the single word as she could. "If someone is waiting in the shadows, I'd be a sitting duck. I'm much safer staying with you all. I'll keep to the back."

"Or maybe," Tanner said at her shoulder, making her jump, "one of our officers could stay with her until we know it's clear."

"Done." Kathy nodded. "Officer Lucas."

"Lieutenant?" The young officer from the Sutter Springs Police Department approached. Fran barely knew him. He was a recent graduate from the academy.

"You stay with our forensic artist until we know the scene is safe."

"Cindy and I will stay here, also," the K-9 handler commented, indicating the dog at her side. "I don't want to mess with any evidence unless you need us."

Officer Lucas nodded. "Yes, Lieutenant."

Fran narrowed her eyes at him. He didn't appear bothered to be her guard. When the young man caught her scrutiny, he nodded with a slight smile.

"Don't worry, ma'am. I'll keep you safe."

She bit back a smile and thanked him. Then she tamped down a sigh. She would much rather be with the group going into the house, but she let it drop.

Grudgingly, Fran backed up to the car and leaned against the front hood. A chilly breeze played with her hair. She crossed her arms at her chest and kept her sights on the officers knocking on the front door. When no one answered, they broke through the door and entered in point formation. She shivered. It wasn't totally a reaction to the drop in temperature. Some of those people were friends. Like Kathy, who always had her back and who had befriended her so long ago, when all she'd wanted to do was to close herself off and wallow in her grief.

Her thoughts moved on to Tanner. When she'd first met him, he hadn't affected her at all. His presence had been more of an annoyance than a temptation. In the past day, though, he'd suddenly become important to her. She hadn't met many men since Sean's death who she felt she could trust. Tanner, though, she knew in her soul, would stand in front of a bullet for her.

That sobering fact shook her.

The last of the officers entered the abandoned house. All of them brave men and women. And all of them risking their lives.

The seconds ticked by while they waited, unspeaking. Cindy sat at attention, completely still. It unnerved her, it seemed so unreal.

The only sound came from the gawking crowd. She ignored the murmurs and nervous laughter.

An officer she wasn't familiar with burst through the door. Just like an overexcited rookie.

"Lieutenant Sawyer!" he called out. "We need you and Cindy. And the forensic artist."

The handler gave Cindy a quiet command. The three of them approached the officer. Tanner stepped out and joined them on the porch.

"I've called the crime scene unit. We need to search the

house and the yard, hopefully before dark. No one is here, but there's blood. And lots of it. We're looking for a body."

Fran's stomach fell. If they found a body, whose would it be? Would they find Darcy? Or were there more victims to this evil?

Tanner had been expecting to find something in the house. Every hair had stood up on the back of his neck the instant they'd burst through the broken door. The inside wasn't anything out of the ordinary. It looked like a house that anyone might live in.

Still. There'd been an odor in the air that had set his pulse racing, ice rushing through his veins. He'd smelled death too many times not to recognize it. Someone had died in this house. Discovering dried blood on a floor in the back bedroom had only confirmed it.

They hadn't even tried to clean it up. That was odd, considering the spic-and-span condition of the kitchen. No doubt, they'd abandoned this house soon after. How long had Joey been kept here?

He knew none of the blood had belonged to the kid. He'd been traumatized but uninjured when he'd showed up on Fran's front lawn. Why and how he and Jared had ended up there remained a mystery.

Tanner hated mysteries. He wanted a bullet-point list of what had happened, when it had occurred and who'd done it. That was just the way he was wired. Walking slowly along the edges of the room, he scanned for any other hints about what had taken place in the room or the identity of the victim.

Or victims.

That amount of blood, he couldn't discount multiple people being killed. He stayed out of the way of the police officers in the small space.

Moving from the bedroom, he immediately found Francesca, tucked into the corner of the room, her pencil rapidly scratching across the page in her sketchpad. He didn't need to see her work to know it would be accurate down to the smallest detail. He hadn't been aware that she had been called in.

"Why are you bothering with that?" the young cop, Officer Lucas, asked, his voice genuinely curious. "The crime scene unit is on their way. They always take pictures."

She didn't take her eyes from the scene. "They do an excellent job. But pictures take in the scene a bit at a time. Using a drawing with the pictures will help the investigators get a better idea of how everything is connected, and may help figure out a timeline. Trust me, I know you don't always have the luxury of both. But after this many cops and a K-9 officer go through a scene, you want to have photos and the drawing."

Tanner nodded. She wasn't wrong. Law enforcement always tried to avoid contaminating a scene. Sometimes, though, it was nearly impossible. And they were human. He'd seen evidence thrown out of court because of carelessness, such as dropping a gum wrapper at the scene. You couldn't take too many precautions.

Tanner tuned the conversation out. He had a crime scene to deal with. And if there was a chance of finding Darcy alive, time was of the essence.

Cindy swept through the house and padded into the room he'd recently vacated. Lieutenant Sawyer gave her a command to "seek."

Within seconds, the large dog left the bedroom and began sniffing through the house. There wasn't a hint of hesitation as the K-9 wandered around the kitchen and then stopped at the back door. Raising one paw, she scratched gently.

"She's on to something. Outside."

All talking ceased. Cindy became the star, leading them all out back. They traipsed around the outside of the two-car garage and past what had once been a woodshed. Unlike the house, it was falling into disrepair. Rounding the corner, Tanner's heart lurched. A pile of freshly turned soil lay beyond the woodshed, a patch of rich, dark brown earth churned and broken, surrounded by undisturbed ground covered with sparse grass. Almost like someone had been tilling land for a garden.

Except it was August, not May. And the small plot was not large enough for a garden, no matter how humble.

It was large enough to bury a body, though.

Tanner wanted to grab a shovel and begin digging. Urgency pounded inside him. He shoved his hands into his pockets and planted himself next to Francesca. There was a procedure to follow.

Within moments, grim officers had their hands gloved and were carefully marking the area with crime scene tape. Once that was completed, they waited for the CSU to arrive and process the scene. No one had any idea how long it would take them to arrive. It all depended on whether or not they were working another scene.

"Will we leave?" Francesca asked him.

He shook his head. "This is connected with a federal case. We'll stay out of their way, but I want to remain on scene."

It seemed to take forever for the CSU to arrive, but in reality, it was less than an hour. Kathy and Officer Lucas remained on scene, as did Lieutenant Sawyer and Cindy.

The CSU had requested they remain in case they found a body and wanted to search for more. Having the K-9 on hand would make the task easier.

Soon, the silent CSU members were digging up the new grave. Francesca stood to the side, gnawing on her bottom lip. Her pencil twitching in her hand. Other than those two signs of agitation, she appeared as calm as a pond on a breezeless summer's day. He was learning her tells, though.

"I have something," a young woman with a CSU coat called out.

He inched closer to the officers. The first thing he saw was an arm. He swallowed bile. It looked youthful. The hand had no wrinkles. Within moments, a young girl, maybe eighteen or nineteen, was uncovered. Her dark blue dress was a familiar design. They left her in her grave while pictures were taken.

"She's Amish," Francesca murmured at his side. He started. He hadn't heard her approach.

Carefully, the CSU worker leaned over the body with a small brush and gently scraped the dirt away. A second later, a dingy *kapp* with a dark stain, like ink or food coloring, on the back, was uncovered.

"Do you think she's Joey's mother?" he asked her.

"Maybe. Or an older sister." She turned to him. Her big amber eyes were damp, but she kept the tears in. "Tanner, can you get a picture for me? I left my phone in Kathy's car. I want to draw her image. Showing a photo of her like this would only hurt Joey. It's better if he sees a drawing of just her face."

He nodded and snapped a picture. She could draw it later if necessary. Although, he didn't see why she would need a photo. Like she'd ever be able to not see the image before them?

"I called the coroner," the CSU team leader announced. "He'll be here in under fifteen."

"Sir, would you like Cindy to search further out?" Lieutenant Sawyer asked.

"Yes. I've got a hunch there's more to find."

Lieutenant Sawyer gave a soft command and the dog set off. Five minutes later, she spoke again.

"Cindy's got something else," Lieutenant Sawyer said.

The entire team turned in unison to watch the German shepherd. She continued sniffing, moving closer to the wooded area at the edge of the property. The K-9 shuffled past the first group of trees then halted. She lifted her tan muzzle and gave an excited bark.

"She found something," Sawyer said, jogging over to her canine partner. Officer Lucas followed behind.

The officers kept their distance while the CSU team members broke the soil with their shovels and picks. This time the ground was hard. Whatever Cindy had found, it hadn't been buried recently.

By the time they'd displaced the top layer of dirt, the coroner arrived. Unlike the Sutter Springs coroner, he drove a large van.

"Bob," the CSU team leader greeted the man. "We might have a second body, unfortunately."

"Understood. I'll start with the first one." He squatted next to the grave and began his investigation. More pictures were snapped.

It didn't take long for the coroner to declare her death a homicide. "I'm going to have the remains transported. She wasn't killed here." He pointed to the blood stains on her dress. "She'd stopped bleeding by the time she was placed in this grave. If her dress had still been wet, the dirt would have stained her dress more."

Respectfully, he gathered the remains of the poor Amish girl and transported her to the back of his vehicle.

Tanner said a prayer that they'd be able to locate her family. They'd be devastated, but they deserved closure. He couldn't imagine the grief and fear they were currently suffering. Not knowing would be a festering wound.

Once they knew, they'd still suffer. But at least they'd know her pain was over. There was a small slice of peace in that knowledge.

The coroner returned to wait and see if the CSU discovered a second corpse.

"We have a body," the CSU member announced. "A female. I'd judge her to be in her forties. She's well preserved, although her face has been damaged beyond recognition. And there's still some clothing."

Tanner's gut twisted. He was close enough to get a peek at the body. Her face had been mangled and her hair color, between the dirt and the dried blood, was matted and impossible to label with a color. If there were clothes with the remains, they had to be under a year old. Instinct told him they'd found Darcy Murray. A DNA test would confirm it.

If it was her, had Jared known what had happened to his mother?

The coroner moved to the second grave. It didn't take long for him to announce the woman buried in the unmarked grave had also been murdered. He gently examined the head and declared she'd died from a single gunshot wound to the face. That explained how her features had been destroyed.

The officers and CSU members stood back in silent respect while this body was transported to the back of the coroner's van, along with the young Amish girl. The coroner got into the front seat and drove away.

They were done here.

The back of his neck prickled.

Tanner spun around, his gaze scanning the area, searching for whoever was watching them. He couldn't see anyone. Even the crowds that had gathered earlier had dissipated.

"What is it?" Kathy asked.

He shrugged, still searching for the danger. "I think someone's out there, but I can't see them."

Francesca stood alone next to the first unearthed grave. She was way too vulnerable out in the open like that.

"Fran!" he called.

"What?"

He opened his mouth to ask her to join them. The sun glinted off something. He caught a glimpse of the long barrel of a rifle pointed in her direction.

"Sniper! Get down!"

Crack! The dirt at Francesca's feet exploded with the force of the bullet's impact. Francesca dove into the open grave a mere second before the second shot fired. This time, he didn't see where it landed.

Had it hit her? Tanner's SIG Sauer was out and in his hand. Kathy and Officer Lucas had their weapons ready too.

Tanner inched forward, his weapon aimed at the trees shrouding the next-door neighbor's lawn.

"Someone needs to check the neighbors. Have they been harmed?"

Right now, he didn't doubt the person, or persons, responsible for the heinous acts they'd discovered since Jared's body had turned up would have any issue with killing a few more innocent people in the pursuit of their own agenda.

What that might be, he still didn't know. All he knew

was that he would willingly give his own life to protect Francesca and any of the innocents in this villain's sights.

He was done playing games. Tanner had a reputation for being mild-mannered. That ended now. Seeing Francesca dive headfirst into an open grave—one that moments before had contained the body of a young woman brutally murdered—had ripped away any desire to stand back and watch others go after the killer.

This one was his.

SEVEN

Fran spat out a mouthful of dirt. Mixed with the soil, the metallic taste of blood lingered on her tongue. She'd bitten it when she hit the bottom of the grave. Thankfully, she wasn't sharing the empty pit with a corpse. She shuddered. The image of the young girl's body in that shallow grave had been branded into her brain. She'd never forget the sight. While she'd worked with skeletal remains in the past, Fran's work didn't often take her to scenes while a subject was being excavated. Gingerly, she sat up. More bits of crumbled earth fell from her hair.

Who had shot at her? If Tanner hadn't shouted to her, she'd have been hit. She'd turned at his holler.

Where was Tanner? And Kathy? And all the other brave souls searching the yard, including Cindy. She held her breath and listened but couldn't make out any noises over the blood pumping in her ears.

She started to rise, keeping her body close to the wall of the grave. A bullet struck the opposite edge, causing a small section of the side to collapse. Ducking back down, she peered at the damage. A hole, six inches in diameter, surrounded the copper-colored bullet lodged in thickly packed dirt. A worm fell from the crater to the floor.

Had she been standing a moment ago, it may have sunk

into her skull. She didn't know how she'd survived so many close calls in less than twenty-four hours. It was like watching a bad horror movie on repeat, always knowing more fear and gore was coming, but unable to stop it.

She didn't even have her cell phone on her, having left it in Kathy's cruiser. There was nothing she could do other than wait the sniper out.

That wasn't completely true. She could still pray. The hurt skeptic inside her scoffed at the notion. Sure, she believed in God. But right now, she didn't even know what words to use.

When she was younger, and still believed good always won over evil, prayer had come so easily to her. She'd felt like she and God had a personal connection. A relationship that assured her she could reach out to Him any time she needed to and He would come to her rescue, like He had for Daniel in the lion's den. That had all changed after Sean had been killed. The connection seemed severed. Or maybe she'd shut God out. Fran still believed God heard her prayers. It had grown little harder to ask Him for what she needed. Partly because she wasn't sure that He was there for her anymore. If He'd ever really been. After all, He had let her husband die. And He had taken her baby, not to mention the fact that she had lost her family due to their prejudices and stubborn clinging to social status. What kind of God allowed that stuff to happen?

Deep in her soul, she knew that God was there. It was the only thing that had sustained her through the hard months after losing her husband. No one else had supported her while she'd mourned. Not even her sister had come to the funeral. Fran had emailed her and had received no response. The hurt caused by that had broken her already devastated heart.

Lord, please help us. Help Tanner and Kathy. Just help. It was all she could think of to say.

She huddled against the wall. Another gunshot rang out, the loud bang echoing in the stillness. She covered her head with her arms, making herself as small as possible. The way she'd done as a kid when practicing tornado drills in the hallway.

Except this was no drill.

Another gunshot. This one followed by an agonized yelp. Was that Tanner? No, she didn't think so, but she had never heard him yell before. Would she recognize his voice when he was in pain? Whoever it was, they'd been struck by the sniper's fire. Pounding footsteps came from beyond the grave in which she cowered.

In the distance, a siren blared.

More police were on the way. Then the keeling wail of an ambulance blasted the silence. Fran swallowed hard. She knew what that meant. Someone was hurt. Hopefully, the coroner wouldn't need to come for a third body. Until she escaped from this hole, there was no way to know who or how bad. Her heart ached fiercely for whoever it was.

"Francesca!" a blessedly familiar voice hissed down to her. Raising her head, her gaze landed on Tanner's head poking into the hole, his bright red hair rumpled like he'd been running a comb through it backward. It reminded her of a spooked cat. His spectacles were filthy. He must have army-crawled to her and was lying on his belly.

"Tanner! Get away from here! He'll shoot you."

He shook his head. "I'm pretty sure he's gone or arrested by now. Didn't you hear the sirens?"

She nodded then remembered. "Oh! I heard the ambulance."

A shadow crossed his face. "Yeah. Officer Lucas was hit. He's already on an ambulance."

She swallowed, holding the greasy nausea at bay.

"Will he be alright?"

"I think so. Listen, let's get you out of there, and I'll tell you everything."

She wanted to be independent, but there was no way she'd be able to climb out of the hole without assistance. The sides had no footholds. And the earth was too crumbly.

"Here. Take my hands." He raised himself to a crouch and reached down to her. She stretched out her arms. Her fingertips touched his palms. He gripped her hands. "Hang on."

When he lifted her, she squeezed his hands and planted her feet against the side of the wall. The bottoms of her boots kept slipping and sliding. She ended up crawling up the side on her knees as he hauled her toward him.

Near the top of the pit, he stood and yanked her the rest of the way. She flew out as if propelled, and slammed into him.

"Oof!" Tanner gasped, stumbling over his feet as her sudden weight shoved him back. He let go of her to wrap his hands protectively around her a second before they tumbled and hit the ground.

Tanner turned to take the brunt of the force and landed on his left shoulder. He grunted at the sudden pain. When Francesca fell on top of him, blinding agony hit him like a fire. For a moment, he could neither breathe nor see. White noise filled his ears.

"Tanner! Tanner!" Francesca's voice came from a distance, almost muffled.

"What?" he groaned. His shoulder continued to throb and burn.

"Open your eyes, Tanner. Please."

Was she crying? He dragged his lids open, blinking as his eyes watered. When his vision cleared, Francesca's welcome face appeared. As well as a large group of cops and two paramedics. Whoa.

"What happened?"

"You blacked out," one of the paramedics responded, making a shooing motion. The others all backed away. Francesca's face vanished. "You've dislocated your shoulder. We need to get you to the hospital, stat."

"Can't you just pop it back in?" He'd been in pain with the bruised ribs. This was almost beyond his endurance.

The other EMT grinned, although sympathy radiated from her face. "You've watched too much TV. Putting a shoulder back needs to be done with care. We don't want to injure you further. You want to use that shoulder again in the future. And you'll need to be sedated. We'll immobilize it, then take you to the ER where you'll be properly cared for. Do you consent to be transported?"

Tanner grimaced. Like he had a choice. He couldn't walk around with a dislocated shoulder. "Yeah."

"We'll need to immobilize your arm."

This was going to hurt.

The two paramedics gathered nearer. They moved quickly, lifting his arm close to his chest then wrapping it in place. He very nearly passed out again. Immediately, the searing torture lessened to a dull ache. He could handle that.

"Thanks." His voice was raw.

"Don't thank us yet. You still need to get that shoulder put back."

Tanner's head sank to the grass. He closed his eyes again while he waited for the paramedics to bring the stretcher. It seemed like only a second when they lifted him from the ground and began wheeling him toward the ambulance. Exhaustion swept over him. Something edged into his consciousness, keeping him from succumbing to sleep.

"Francesca." He fought to stay awake. He needed to talk with her.

"I'm here, Tanner."

The unease melted away. She was there. She was safe. "Stick with Kathy. I'll come see you as soon as they fix me up."

"Relax, cowboy. I'll be fine. When you're up to it, we'll talk and plan our next step."

Sighing, he released the final strands of tension holding him awake. He'd tell her about everything when he was better. Until then, Kathy would see to her.

It seemed like only minutes later when he felt himself being lifted from the back of the ambulance. The jolt of the wheels hitting the pavement sent pain coursing through his shoulder and arm, robbing him of his breath. The paramedics steered him through the sliding doors. Every bump and crack in the pavement and floor vibrated through him. Tanner clenched his teeth to keep from embarrassing himself with another groan.

Soon, his aching jaw joined the growing list of body parts that hurt.

"We're almost there," the female EMT murmured near his head.

He didn't trust himself to speak, so he nodded to show he'd heard and understood her message. Only one thought distracted him from his current situation.

Where was Francesca? Had she gone back to the station? Was she with Kathy, as he'd asked, or had her independent streak taken over? With her, one could never tell.

The paramedics dropped him off in a curtained cubicle

and departed, leaving him to the mercy of a rather harassed-looking nurse. He'd never seen a nurse seem so frazzled. Regardless of her appearance, she performed her duties efficiently, taking his vital signs and recording them on the laptop she placed on the cart near the bed.

"The doctor will be right in," she told him, picking up the laptop. She walked toward the entrance. The curtain was pulled back and Francesca entered, trailed by Kathy.

Relief surged, helping him forget the pain for a moment.

"Francesca! I wondered where you were."

Kathy's eyebrows climbed her forehead.

"What?"

"I've never heard anyone call her Francesca." She frowned at the younger woman. "I'd practically forgotten it was your real name."

Francesca shrugged, her cheeks glowing pink. "My parents liked old-fashioned names. My sister Stacy's full name is Anastasia."

Tanner squirmed as much as his injured shoulder allowed. He hadn't meant anything by calling her Francesca. It just seemed to suit her better than Fran. When he thought of Fran, his mind conjured images of an elderly lady crocheting blankets. Francesca seemed more fitting to an elegant young woman.

"If it bothers you, I'll call you Fran."

He didn't want to. He liked having a name that only he used. He tried not to think about that too deeply.

The corners of her lips tilted up at the ends. "I don't mind. It's only a name."

It was more than that. A name was a highly personal part of one's identity. However, he was suffering too much for any kind of philosophical discussion.

The curtain opened again, interrupting their conversation. The emergency room doctor entered. "I hear we need to reset a shoulder."

Kathy stepped forward. "We'll go now. I just wanted to make sure all was well."

He met Kathy's eyes, trying to plead with her silently to stay with Francesca.

"Call me tomorrow when you feel well enough to work," the woman in question said. "I want to go and check on Joey to see if he can give us anything more. I should have the sketch of the girl by then."

He heard what she didn't say. She wanted to know if Joey knew or could help them find out who the two bodies they'd found belonged to. His gut told him the skeleton was all that remained of Darcy Murray, although he wouldn't say that in front of a stranger. Tomorrow, they'd begin the search for any missing Amish teenagers, as well as expand the search for Joey's family.

It would be a grueling day.

"I'm going to hang out with Fran tonight," Kathy responded to his unspoken plea. "We'll have a girls' night."

Francesca looked annoyed but, to his relief, she didn't protest.

Regardless, he knew he wouldn't stop worrying until the threat was eliminated.

EIGHT

"I'm not sure we should have left him like that," Fran muttered as she buckled the seat belt.

"Relax." Kathy threw her long-suffering glance. "You act so tough and prickly, but you have the softest heart of anyone I've ever met. Tanner will be fine. It's a dislocated shoulder. Nothing life-threatening. And by now, he's sound asleep. So there's no reason for us to hang around."

Fran huffed, looking out the window. It was a clear evening. The moon glowed warmly in the sky. Here in the city, barely any stars were visible. When they got to her house, though, the dark sky would be a glittering mass of stars. It was one of the reasons she'd fallen in love with the place so long ago. She'd never minded the seclusion. Sutter Springs was a close-knit community. She'd always felt safe there.

Until now.

Had it only been this morning that she'd found a body in her yard? A shiver wracked her spine. She'd caught the glance Kathy and Tanner had exchanged. Normally, she would have complained about being managed. She was a grown woman, and a widow. She'd been on her own for a long time and could take care of herself.

It was a sign of how rattled she was that she hadn't. In fact, she welcomed Kathy's presence tonight.

"I need to get a dog."

Kathy laughed. "Where did that come from?"

Fran chuckled. "I was thinking out loud. If I had a dog, I wouldn't feel quite so anxious about being alone in my house."

"Fran, I'll stay tonight."

"Yeah, I know. But you can't put your life on hold to play babysitter for me. No matter how many times Special Agent Tanner Hall gives you that puppy-dog look and begs you to."

"You caught that?"

Fran snorted. "Please, it was hard to miss. Neither of you were exactly subtle."

"You need protection for a bit. It's no trouble."

Fran's stomach muscles grew tight when her house came into view. It didn't look any different than normal, but there seemed to be something sinister about the shadows as the lights of the cruiser beamed along the driveway.

"I almost expected to see the crime scene tape."

"It's already been processed."

Fran waited until the car was turned off before she opened her door and placed her foot on the gravel driveway. She'd taken two steps toward her home when her motion-detecting lights came on, flooding the first few feet of the yard and the front of the house. The light illuminated the porch, but the shadows beyond seemed lengthened.

"It's creepy out here. Let's go inside."

Kathy didn't argue. When they reached the house, though, she insisted on checking the place first before letting Fran enter. Fran double-checked all the locks.

"I'm setting my alarm for six." She handed Kathy a clean towel and a washcloth. "Go ahead and take a shower. You're in the front guest room."

Kathy had stayed over before and knew which room she was talking about.

"Sounds good. I will be getting up every hour to sweep the place and make sure all is well. I think having my black-and-white in the driveway should be a good preventive should anyone want to break in."

Fran nodded. She wasn't completely confident but having Kathy around did help. She'd feel better if it were Tanner.

Instantly, she flushed and turned away to hide it. It seemed almost like a betrayal of Kathy to admit she felt safer with the quiet FBI agent than with her extremely competent friend. A friend, she reminded herself, who had been decorated multiple times for her bravery in the line of work. She was in good hands with Kathy on the premises.

As she pulled back the blanket that night, Fran took a moment to sink to her knees beside the bed. The chill from the wooden floor penetrated her pajamas and sank into her skin. She ignored the discomfort and took a few minutes to thank God for his continued protection. She prayed for Joey, Kathy, Officer Lucas and Tanner. Satisfied that she'd done all she could, she rose and slid under the covers. Despite the heat of the day, the evening air had a definite bite to it.

She didn't think she'd be able to fall asleep, so much had happened that day. The trauma had taken its toll, however. Exhaustion soon pulled her under into a deep dreamless sleep.

Fran jerked awake sometime later. It took her a moment to get her bearings. She was in her room…but what had awakened her?

Moonlight poured through the slats of the blinds. It was still the middle of the night. Her stomach growled. She hadn't eaten dinner. That must have been what had woken her. Glancing at the clock on the table beside her bed, she groaned. Four fifty-six. For an instant, she debated trying to grab that extra hour of sleep before the alarm went off. Her stomach rumbled viciously in protest.

Food it was.

Slipping her legs over the edge of the mattress, she stood and grabbed her robe. She slid her feet into her slippers and padded out into the hall toward the kitchen. She'd just grab a piece of toast and a glass of water, then go back to bed. Something quick that wouldn't make a mess she'd need to clean up in the morning.

She passed the front guest bedroom and paused, frowning. Kathy's alarm was going off. She waited, but her friend made no effort to silence it. The panic started to curdle in her gut when she heard Kathy snore and mumble in her sleep.

Fran snickered. Kathy would never believe she talked in her sleep, but Fran had heard it before. Should she wake her up? After a minute, the alarm died on its own. Fran hesitated for another moment. No. She'd let Kathy sleep. After all, she was wide awake. If she needed to, she'd wake Kathy after she ate.

She continued to the kitchen and turned on the single light above the sink. It wasn't very bright, but it gave off enough light to serve her purpose. She made herself some toast and, on the way to the sink, changed her mind. Who was she fooling? She would never be able to go back to sleep. Grabbing her teakettle, she refreshed the water and set it on the stove. Then she chose her favorite salted-caramel tea. Ten minutes later, her stomach satisfied, she took her steaming mug and went into the den.

This was one of her favorite rooms in the house. It was a workspace, but it was also cozy and roomy enough for two ceiling-high bookcases. It gave her a sense of peace. She used to come here for her morning devotional. She'd gotten out of the habit. The desire to take it up again hit her. Maybe she would. It was time she put effort into her relationship with God. She took a cautious sip of her tea, her gaze roaming the familiar space. Her eyes paused on the old disreputable chair in the corner. Really, it was nothing more than an eyesore. Sean had claimed to like the wobbly swivel chair, but he'd used a different one at the desk. In fact, had she ever seen him sit in it? It hadn't been a family gift. She recalled him bringing it home, claiming he'd fix it one day.

He never had.

She hadn't been able to remove it, but she knew she wouldn't fix it. It was ugly and superfluous. She had more than enough chairs. That was it. It was way past time for the chair to go.

Her mug thunked on the desk when she set it down. She marched to the chair and grabbed the arms, fully intending to drag the unwanted furniture from the room. When she yanked on it, however, it tipped and the seat fell off, revealing a hidden compartment she'd never known about. One that flipped open to reveal a small wooden box inside.

Her breath froze in her chest. There was no chance Sean hadn't known about the compartment. She'd given him that box on his birthday the year they'd married. He'd said he'd lost it in the move. He'd lied. And he'd kept secrets from her.

Her hand trembled as she reached for the box. She tapped out the password by heart: 0830. The day they met at college. The lid clicked and popped open. She didn't know what she'd expected to see inside. It definitely wasn't a meticulously kept bank register. One with two hundred and thirty thousand dollars in it. In Sean's name. She dropped into the desk chair, dazed. There'd been no small deposits.

All of them were for ten-, twenty- or fifty-thousand dollars. All from CR. Who was CR?

Tanner. She needed to show this to Tanner. He'd know what to do. Plus, maybe it something Sean had been working on for his job with the FBI. She held that wish close to her heart. She could handle that better than the obvious conclusion that her husband had been dirty.

A noise in the hall alerted her to someone moving about. Kathy probably felt guilty about sleeping through her alarm. Fran dropped the box into a desk drawer then left the den.

In the hall, she paused, frowning when she didn't see her friend.

The skin between her shoulder blades prickled. Spinning, she peered into the darkness.

A hand clapped over her mouth, holding in her scream. A second arm stole across her torso. In the moonlight, something glinted.

Her attacker held a knife.

She was trapped in the embrace of a killer. One determined to end her life.

Why wasn't Kathy answering her cell phone? Something was wrong. Tanner knew Kathy's reputation, even if he didn't know her very well. She was diligent, by the book, and fiercely capable. That was the only reason he'd been comfortable leaving her in charge of protecting Francesca.

She'd been texting him every hour on the hour, just to let him know that she'd checked the perimeter and had seen nothing out of the ordinary.

He'd relaxed, knowing that Francesca was in good hands.

Until the moment he'd been discharged and had tried to text Kathy for the latest update so he could go back to his hotel room and relax until 7:00 a.m.

Kathy had never responded. He'd waited with a growing sense of unease for the hour mark to pass. Still no text. He called her next. When the call went to voicemail, sweat broke out on his forehead. That was not Kathy.

He hated bothering Francesca. She needed sleep. But he had to know if she was safe. So, he dialed her number. By the time her voicemail message came on, he was already running. He jumped into the middle of the street and waved down a passing car. Tanner dashed to the driver side window. The young man rolled it down and opened his mouth, clearly irritated. Tanner cut him off and flashed his FBI badge in the young man's face.

"FBI. I need a vehicle. You can drive me or give me the keys. Your choice." He'd never done that before, but he was desperate.

"Get in." Instantly, the young man lost his disgruntled attitude and appeared excited to be part of an FBI operation. Tanner had forgotten what it felt like to be that excited about his job.

Tanner ran around to the passenger side and hopped in, ignoring his complaining shoulder and ribs. This probably wasn't what the doctor had had in mind when he'd said to take it easy for the next couple of days, but Tanner refused to play it safe when Francesca and Kathy were potentially in danger. He'd learned long ago that people needed to be the priority.

Francesca was quickly becoming a high priority for him. But he'd contemplate that later.

"Where am I going?" the driver queried.

Tersely, he gave him the address. The kid plugged it in to the GPS, looking for the quickest route. "We'll take a back road," he informed Tanner, pulling out into traffic. "It'll avoid some higher populated areas and lights. According to my map, it will shave off three minutes."

Lives could be saved in three minutes. Tanner nodded, holding tight to the handle above the window. The car's lights swept through the still-dark sky. The sunrise was minutes away.

It took more patience than he could ever recall possessing to wait for the miles to pass.

Tanner took a deep breath and said a brief prayer. The situation was beyond human control. If Francesca and Kathy were in peril, only He knew what it was. And only God would be able to save them.

Tanner called Dispatch and requested backup. When he was advised to wait before going in, he shook his head.

"Sorry. I can't do that. Miss Brown and Lieutenant Bartlett may be currently in a life-threatening situation. I'm going in." He hung up and kept a close watch on the road, searching for any hidden dangers. Finally, the edge of Francesca's driveway appeared. He didn't want to warn anyone. They might panic and pull the trigger in reaction.

"This is it. Drop me off here and go."

The driver looked distinctly disappointed. "What if you need a ride back?"

"You heard my call. Law enforcement personnel are en route. You'll be in danger if you remain."

The kid nodded reluctantly. Tanner opened the door and jumped out.

Francesca had a long driveway. It would normally take him two or three minutes to walk to her house.

He wasn't planning on walking. Relying on the glow from his flashlight app, Tanner took off and raced the length of the drive, praying the two women in the house were alive, fearing he'd be too late.

NINE

Fran struggled against her attacker's hold, twisting back and forth. He had a good foot and probably fifty pounds on her. But she had a strong desire to live fueling the fury of her fight. If only she'd forgotten her charity toward Kathy and awakened her friend when she'd heard the alarm. If Kathy awoke to discover her body, she'd never forgive herself.

She had to make sure it didn't come to that.

The blade of the knife pushed against the edge of her throat. She fought the urge to swallow, not wanting to increase the pressure.

Her attacker cursed and pressed harder. While it hurt, the knife wasn't sharp enough to do the job. He was unprepared to slit her throat, although strong enough to stab her if he decided to take that route. She needed to throw him off balance.

Recalling something she'd read once, Fran grabbed the muscular arm holding the knife with both hands and picked her feet up off the floor.

Caught off balance, he pitched forward. When he dropped her to stop his fall, the sleeve she was holding on to tore. A moment later, she landed on one knee in the middle of the dim hallway.

She couldn't stay there. Shaking off her daze, she jumped

to her feet and dashed toward the front door. She undid the dead bolt and the chain, fingers shaking. Ripping the heavy door open, she charged out into the early morning. The barest hint of pink lit the horizon line.

A faint *whoosh* was her only warning. She leaped to the right, deflecting the knife from the middle of her back. She took the hit near her shoulder instead. A blazing pain seared through her. She staggered, falling down the porch steps.

Before she could rise a second time, her assailant was on her again. He yanked his knife from her shoulder. She had only a second before he'd stab her again. Pinned to the ground, her face shoved into the gravel, she couldn't fight it.

Tensing, she waited for the final blow, hoping her death wouldn't be too painful.

A shot rang out. The man holding her down shouted. The knife clattered to the stones next to her head.

"FBI! Hands in the air where I can see them," Tanner's welcome voice bellowed. Fran didn't know how he'd managed to arrive at the perfect time, nor did she care. She was alive.

The weight holding her to the ground stumbled off. Literally. The tall man who'd been so determined to kill her mere seconds earlier rose and tripped over her before sprinting for the back of the house.

Tanner raised the gun and shouted again. The killer kept going.

As soon as Tanner had secured the attacker, she'd go inside and check on Kathy. She couldn't distract Tanner and endanger them both. Only the recollection of her friend mumbling in her sleep reassured her.

Fran raised her head in time to see her would-be assassin disappear into the shadows. She hadn't gotten a good glimpse of him. She had seen some sort of tattoo on his right biceps, the arm that had held the knife. The sleeve she'd ripped had hung to his wrist and dropped to the ground. He'd left it behind.

Although she'd never had a clear image, she'd had caught some red and green. Maybe a dinosaur or a dragon. Remembering the picture Tanner had showed her of the house where they'd found the bodies yesterday, she recalled the impression of someone standing in the window with some kind of tattoo. She couldn't be positive that it was the same man, but it seemed too coincidental not to be. They didn't have a name, but they had part of his clothing, so there would be DNA evidence.

Not to mention his blood was on the handle of the knife he'd dropped when Tanner shot it out of his hand. Her gaze flicked to the weapon. She shuddered. Her blood ran wet on the blade.

Tanner shot toward the darkness again. But instead of giving chase, he ran to her side and dropped down near her injured shoulder. Before she could even greet him or ask him what he was doing there, he'd shed his jacket and was pressing it against the wound in her shoulder blade.

The sudden agony shut out all other thoughts. She grunted.

"I'm sorry, Francesca. I know it hurts, but I have to stop the bleeding." He held the jacket against her back with one hand and fumbled for his phone with the other.

The intense pain continued, but she fought against it to remain conscious. She was the only witness to the events.

And she needed to tell Tanner about Kathy.

She listened to him call Dispatch. He asked for an ambulance. She winced. Again. And the police. Thankfully, no coroner this time.

"Tanner. Kathy…"

"Is she alright? I have been trying her cell phone for the past hour. That's why I came out so early."

"I think she slept past her alarm. Not like her." Why was she so tired? "I'm worried about her."

"I'll check on her in a moment. As soon as the ambulance crew arrives. I don't dare leave you out here by yourself. You get yourself into enough trouble without me."

"Ha, ha." Fran closed her eyes. He was trying to keep her spirits up. She understood it and appreciated it. She didn't want to admit how much it relieved her having him at her side. Nor did she relish the notion that he'd abandon her to the very capable paramedics. But Kathy concerned her. The conscientious cop she knew would not sleep through an alarm, and definitely not the ruckus of the past twenty minutes. Something was wrong.

In her mind, she recalled getting herself a cup of tea. There had been an empty mug in the sink.

"Kathy slept though her alarm and all this noise. Not like her. I could be wrong," she slurred, breaking off to yawn before speaking further, "but I think she drank something in the middle of the night. What if he poisoned her?"

It was a long shot, but she couldn't deny the feeling that her attacker was also responsible for Kathy's lack of vigilance.

Tanner nodded. At the wail of a siren, his head jerked up. In a moment, he'd be gone.

"Tanner. In my desk in the den, left side, the large drawer. There's a small wooden box. The combination is 0830. I found it and think it might be important. Maybe related to Sean's work. Can you get it and look at it after Kathy?"

"Don't worry, Francesca. I won't forget. I'll come by and see you as soon as I can, and we can talk about it."

It was all the time they had before the ambulance arrived and took over.

The last thing she saw before she closed her eyes was Tanner sprinting away. He paused at the top of the porch steps and glanced back at her, his blue eyes piercing behind his glasses. Then he bolted inside the house.

She felt colder without him at her side. Sighing, she let sleep claim her.

The second he verified that Francesca was safely being loaded onto the ambulance, Tanner hightailed it into the house. The second siren of the arriving police backup reassured him further.

Holding his SIG Sauer at the ready, he moved from room to room, making sure the assassin hadn't circled back and reentered the house. In the small dining alcove next to the kitchen, the sliding screen door stood wide open. It didn't take long to determine it had been forced and the lock was busted. He snapped a picture.

"Police!"

"Sergeant Beck, back here."

Two sets of footsteps clomped over the hardwood stairs. Sergeant Steve Beck and Officer Melissa McCoy appeared in the doorway.

"Special Agent Hall," Officer McCoy addressed him.

"Officer McCoy. Sergeant Beck. You made good time." He nodded once. "Let's get down to business. We have forced entry here. The unsub attacked Francesca Brown with a knife." Both officers inhaled sharply. "She's on her way to the hospital now. I don't believe any vital organs were affected. My main concern is that Lieutenant Kathy Bartlett has not responded to phone calls, her alarm, or sounds of gunfire. Francesca said she's still asleep but is concerned it's not a natural sleep."

"I'll start looking for any evidence of foul play here," Melissa volunteered.

Tanner shook his head. "No. If Kathy is still asleep, she'll not appreciate being awakened by a couple of guys, even if we are friends."

"Go," Steve said. "I'll search the house and start taking pictures."

"Check each room. I've only gotten this far, and the unsub might be on scene. Or a partner if he had help."

That settled, Tanner and Melissa separated. He continued into the next room. A few minutes later, Melissa called to him from another room. He walked in to find her trying to wake Kathy.

"This isn't natural, sir. Lieutenant Bartlett is a notorious light sleeper. I've heard others tease her about it. But nothing I do wakes her."

"How are her vitals?"

She checked her pulse. "Her pulse is strong. And her breathing is slightly heavy. Sir, I think she's been drugged."

"I agree." Sliding his phone from his front pocket, he called for a second ambulance. Once he'd explained the emergency and had hung up, he returned his phone to his pocket. "It might not be an emergency, but if she is drugged, I don't know what or how much she's been given."

By the time the ambulance crew arrived, Kathy still wasn't stirring. The paramedics worked efficiently. Tanner got out of their way and left the room. He took two steps toward the kitchen before remembering what Francesca had whispered to him before she'd been wheeled away.

Pivoting, he marched toward the den. Whatever she'd found had concerned her. For the life of him, he couldn't think of a single thing that Sean could have been working on that he'd have evidence at home. His colleague had never liked bringing files home, and preferred working overtime to clear his desk at the office rather than face offsite work.

Obviously, Francesca hadn't wanted anyone else to see what she'd found. He'd respect that. If it was something the police needed to know about, he'd reassess. He doubted that would be necessary. Sean had been one of the most dedicated workers he'd ever known.

A minute later, he sat behind the desk and opened the drawer. The box was nearly the sole object in the large drawer. It weighed only a few ounces. He flipped it around and found the small keypad. What had she said the passcode was? He entered the 0830 code and nodded when he heard a soft click. Good. He'd hate to break an obviously handmade box.

Setting it on the desk, he opened it. Then frowned, puzzled. He hadn't expected to find a bank register inside. Why would this concern the FBI?

The moment he started looking at the deposits and balances, something in him jolted to a halt. Sean had been his friend for years. They'd laughed together and had supported each other through some brutal cases. He hadn't had many friends he'd trusted during his life, but Sean had been one.

Right now, there was no doubt in Tanner's mind that his trusted friend had been a dirty agent.

He tried to deny it. Scoured his mind for reasons to explain what he was seeing. The only things he could come up with were bribery, theft and extortion.

None of those gelled with the man he'd known. He hoped he was missing a major clue, but he'd have to turn in these findings so an investigation could be opened.

Would the investigation touch Francesca? She'd given

them to him, expecting him to find the answers. All the entries were in Sean's name.

Glancing at his watch, he decided he had a few moments. He needed to call his SAC. But not while he was in the house with officers who might overhear.

Once Kathy was out of the house, he located Sergeant Beck and Officer McCoy.

"Are you guys good to finish up here? I want to call my SAC and head to the hospital."

Steve waved him away. "Go. We won't be much longer. Tell Fran we're thinking of her."

Melissa added her agreement.

That was done. Tanner made his way outside. Then he recalled he didn't have a vehicle. Grimacing, he pondered the situation. He didn't want to be stuck here until the others were done. Nor did he want to wait until the car rental places opened at ten.

He pulled out his phone and dialed Jack.

"Lo?" Jack answered, his voice still groggy.

"Sorry, man. Didn't want to wake you, but I'm in a bind." Succinctly, he brought Jack up to speed.

"No problem. You know I always have too many vehicles around my place. Nicole and I will come to you. I have the perfect truck for you to use. Consider it a no risk loan until SAC Mitchell supplies you with a replacement."

He appreciated the loan. He'd not sneer at the gift. No risk meant that even if he blew the thing up, Jack wouldn't be upset. As he'd said, Jack did tend to collect vehicles, so he always had one or two to spare.

Fifteen minutes later, Jack rumbled into view in a pickup truck, his wife driving a mid-size sedan behind him. Knowing time was of the essence, they didn't hold him up as he gathered the keys and settled himself in the truck.

He'd use that until a new car was made available to him. Hopefully, later today. He hated using someone else's vehicle. The need to be extra cautious with other people's property had been installed in him and all his siblings since they'd been in diapers. But with a job like his, caution sometimes wasn't enough.

Yesterday's accident was a prime example of that fact. He waited until he was on the road to the hospital before calling his superior.

SAC Mitchell answered on the second ring. "Special Agent Hall. It's only seven in the morning."

He grimaced. Yeah, he had forgotten about the time. Between confronting a killer and finding out Sean had been lying, he felt like he'd put in a full day's work. And he hadn't even eaten breakfast. That meant SAC Mitchell was still at home with her family.

"Sorry, ma'am. But I came across some information I thought needed immediate attention." Sticking to the facts, he recited the list of everything that had occurred since they'd last spoken, keeping a tight rein on his emotions so his anger and feelings of betrayal wouldn't leak into his voice.

She was silent for a long moment when he completed his report.

Then her sigh came down the line. "We'll have to look into the account immediately. If there has been no movement since he died, and if Fran Brown isn't named as a beneficiary on the account, I feel we can clear her of being involved. It's to her credit that she gave the information to you rather than trying to discover the answers herself."

Tanner's hands tightened on the wheel. "So, you think Sean was up to no good."

The fact she'd not denied it immediately told him that his one hope had been blown out of the water.

"I hate to say it, but whatever he was doing, it wasn't sanctioned by us. He was definitely playing with something he shouldn't have been." Her voice hardened. "It may have gotten him killed. And, seeing how Jared showed up on his lawn, it may have been the cause of our witness's death too."

Tanner swallowed hard. He didn't know what his former colleague had been involved in. Their friendship hadn't been as strong as Tanner had thought. Right now, he needed to get past his grief and protect Francesca from paying for her husband's sins like he had—with his life.

TEN

Fran wanted to go home. Technically, she wanted to be anywhere except inside the hospital. She'd woken up about ten minutes ago and had yet to see a single nurse or doctor. Her shoulder ached, but at least it no longer felt like it was on fire. That was the only silver lining she could see in her current situation.

She was in a hospital and had no clue how serious her wound had been. However, judging by the lack of monitors, wires or hovering nurses, she'd be safe in assuming her injuries weren't life-threatening.

They could have been. Had she not jumped when she'd heard the knife, she probably wouldn't have made it to the ambulance.

Thank the Lord, Tanner had been there.

Had he managed to catch the man who'd tried to kill her? And had he found out if this was the same man who had killed the Amish girl and the nameless woman? Maybe he'd learned why Joey had been taken.

Thinking of Joey brought a whole new list of worries. How was the child faring now that he'd been again moved to stay with strangers? Did they understand how devastating disruptions to routines are to children with autism?

It was difficult, but she forced herself not to dwell on

Joey. There was nothing she could do for him. She didn't even know where he was at the moment. All she could do was trust in God's providence. Sometimes that was easier said than done. Especially when there was no proof that her prayers were being answered.

Sometimes faith was as much a personal decision as a spiritual truth.

Fran heard a male voice in the hall. Had Tanner arrived? She pressed the button to raise the back of her bed. When the voice continued past her room, she sighed. How long did she need to stay here anyway? She turned her head to see the clock on the wall. Nearly eleven in the morning. She'd been out for over four hours. Why wasn't Tanner here yet?

The acid in her stomach churned and the muscles cramped. She pressed a hand against it in a useless effort to keep it still. The panic that had simmered below the surface of her consciousness since the moment she'd awakened alone in the hospital began bubbling inside her. Clenching her fists tight, she squeezed her eyes shut. *Focus on deep breathing.* She drew in a slow, deep breath and released it on a shuddering sigh. She was okay. No one would harm her here.

That wasn't really the issue, though. Nor was she panicking from being in the hospital this time. Not completely.

She'd told Tanner about the box in the office. She'd had to. That wasn't something she could keep to herself. But what if telling Tanner had been a mistake? What if he looked into it and discovered Sean was involved with something bad? How would that affect her?

She knew it was selfish, but her job was all that she had that was hers. She didn't have parents or her sister. Her baby and her husband were both gone. While she had friends, she did tend to keep them at a distance.

The door opened. A woman she'd never met entered the

room. She wore her ID badge on a sturdy black lanyard around her neck. The second Fran saw the words Children and Youth, she stiffened.

Whatever they wanted to talk to her about had to involve Joey. Had they found his family? Was he injured, or did they just want to be neighborly and let her know his progress?

Somehow, she doubted it. Something was wrong.

"Miss Brown." The woman approached with a no-nonsense attitude. Fran relaxed slightly. This woman, she felt confident, wouldn't pull any punches. Even if she wasn't bringing good news, she'd tell it to her straight.

"Yes. I'm assuming you're here about Joey."

The woman hesitated. "I'm not sure that is his name."

"He responded when he heard it, so we have been using it." They couldn't keep calling him "the kid," after all.

"I'm not saying it isn't, but it's irrelevant right now. Chief Spencer told me you'd be here. I stopped by the station before I came here."

"Why?" Her stomach quivered. This wasn't good.

"The woman staying with the boy in the hotel called me two hours ago to tell me he'd snuck out. We thought maybe he'd head toward the precinct to find you."

Her breath stuck in her throat. It took her a few horrifying seconds to remember how to breathe. "What do you mean he's gone? How did he get out?"

The woman shifted. "That's unclear."

Fran shoved her blankets to the side. She couldn't stay here while Joey was on his own. She spied her clothes on the chair and grabbed them, grimacing at the bloodstains on her shirt. It was all she had available. Marching into the small bathroom, she threw on her dirty clothes then returned to the room. The social worker was still standing awkwardly near the bed, apparently stumped about what she should do.

What had she expected? Why come to see Fran if she didn't plan on joining the search for Joey? Fran scanned the room until her gaze rested on her shoes. When this was done, those things would join her bloody shirt in the garbage bin and she'd treat herself to something new. Shoes that didn't have the stench of death on them. It didn't matter that they still had wearability. She'd never be able to see them without remembering the details of everything that had happened while she'd worn them. Steeling herself, she slid her feet into them.

Her back throbbed and her head began to ache, but Fran refused to back down. Sometimes you had to overlook physical discomfort to do the right thing.

A nurse entered and halted, her mouth pressed into a determined line. "You haven't been released yet."

"Doesn't matter. I have to help search for a missing child."

The nurse's eyes popped wide open.

"What's this about a missing child?" a welcome voice asked from the door.

Fran's spine melted in relief.

Tanner had arrived. He'd add his support and spring her from this place so they could find Joey.

It concerned her how strongly she was relying on a man who, really, was little more than a stranger.

She'd worry about that later. Right now, she needed Tanner.

Joey was all that mattered.

Francesca turned to face him. The complete trust shining from the glance she beamed at him slammed into him with the force of a two-by-four, almost causing him to stumble where he stood. Tanner had never been the recipient of such total confidence before. The urge to spin on his heel and leave shocked him. He wouldn't, of course, but Tanner had never been more keenly aware of all his faults and his own unworthiness than at that very moment.

He shoved his doubts aside.

"Francesca, did something happen to Joey?"

She nodded and pointed to an unfamiliar woman. "This is the social worker. Joey slipped out during the night. They have no idea where he is."

All other concerns fled. "Gotcha. Are you ready to go?"

"Sir, she can't leave yet." The nurse caught his attention. "She needs to see the doctor."

He scowled. Francesca looked worn, her skin pale and drawn. But also determined. There was no way they'd keep her there. He flashed his FBI badge. Second time since he'd left the hospital several hours earlier. That had to be some kind of record for him.

"Look, do what you need to do. But there's an autistic child out there being hunted by a killer. That woman is the only one he'll allow near him. She has to come with me. It's FBI business."

The nurse clapped her mouth shut and held up one finger before whisking herself out the door.

"Now what?" the social worker huffed.

"Now we wait for her to bring Francesca's release papers."

The nurse brought them, and a doctor, a short time later. She stood in the background, her lips pursed like she was holding in a lot of things she wanted to say but didn't dare. The doctor presented the papers to Francesca and had her sign them.

"The knife wound wasn't deep and it didn't nick any arteries, so it should heal fine. Keep it clean. You were due for a tetanus booster, so I gave you that. I also gave you an antibiotic shot, but you should have this prescription filled as well. Come back if it gets infected. Do you have someone to change the dressing?"

Kathy could do it, he supposed. Francesca would be pleased to know her friend would be fine. Or, if Kathy wasn't available, he could change her dressing if she wore a sleeveless blouse. It was close enough to the top of her arm.

"I do," she said. He wondered if she had thought through the options or was placating the doctor. With Francesca, either could be true.

"All right, young lady. Go find that child. But I want you to rest at the earliest instant."

She nodded her agreement. Tanner bit back a grin. The likelihood of that happening was slim to none, but the doctor didn't need to know everything.

Francesca thanked the doctor and stepped closer to Tanner. Again, her strength amazed him. "Right. Let's go. Thank you, Doctor."

Holding the door open for Francesca and the social worker, he led the way down the corridor and past the security desk. Several people milling around the lobby tossed scandalized looks at Francesca's shirt. He'd have to see to it that she had something clean and whole to wear. He shook his head. That could wait until they found Joey.

"Which hotel were you holed up in?"

When the social worker gave him the name of a locally owned hotel, he did a quick map search on his phone. "That's less than a mile from the precinct. Joey has proved to be incredibly observant. I wouldn't put it past him to make his way back to where he last saw Francesca. Tell you what, you get in your car and we'll get in ours. We'll start from the hotel and work our way out. If you go the op-posite direction, we can cover more ground. I'm guessing there are already officers searching for him?"

"You're correct. Chief Spencer has ordered them to call in if they find the boy. Unless he's in immediate danger, they are to wait for Fran to arrive."

"Makes sense. He'll run from anyone else."

He motioned for Francesca to get into the truck he'd driven.

When he was behind the wheel and driving off the hospital grounds, she spoke the words he'd been expecting since he'd showed up in her room. "How's Kathy?"

"Kathy is great. Sergeant Beck found a syringe near her bed. She'd been given a very strong sedative while she'd slept. Most likely to keep her out of the way while the as-sailant took you out of the picture. The man who attacked you is still at large."

She sighed. "I figured he was. What I don't understand is why they gave Kathy a sedative. Wouldn't it have been more efficient to kill her?"

He curled his lip. "Because we are dealing with cow-ards who take down unarmed women and children. They haven't actually attacked any law enforcement personnel at close range. They've used cars and sniper scopes to do that. I think whoever is calling the shots knows that offing cops would increase the heat. Or maybe they doubt their ability to come out the winner."

"He had a tattoo," she murmured. "I wonder if I can get Joey to draw it."

He gave a silent whistle. "Nice. I hadn't thought of that, but yeah. The kid might have seen it. Something like a tat-too would be a definite way to identify our killer."

His phone rang. He jabbed the button on the console to answer it. "Yeah?"

"Special Agent Hall, this is Sergeant Beck. We've located Joey."

Beside him, Francesca's head dropped into her hands. When her shoulders shook, he winced. She'd been through the wringer. Without thinking, he reached out and rubbed her shoulder. When his hand brushed over dried blood, he froze. Oops. He'd forgotten about her wound. She stilled, but didn't pull away or protest. He returned the hand to the wheel.

"Great news! Where should I bring Francesca?"

"He's right outside the station, hiding behind the shrubbery along the west side of the building."

"We'll be there in five minutes. Let Children Services know, would you?"

"Sure thing."

Francesca lifted her face. Her lashes were wet, but she wasn't crying. "I'm so relieved. You were right. He was headed back to where he'd last seen me."

"It makes sense. You are the only one he's connected with. I am concerned at how easy he ran off."

She nodded. Then she bit her lip. He saw the indecision crawl across her expression.

"I have news about the contents of the box you told me about. But I'd prefer to hold off until we have more time so I can explain it."

"It's bad."

It wasn't a question.

He didn't deny it. It was bad, although they hadn't discovered how bad. But it would be devastating for her to learn about it. The one plus: she had been eliminated as a suspect. That would be one less thing for her to deal with.

The last mile was silent. When they reached the precinct, he stopped along the curb and parked. Why make her trek around the building when the target was twenty feet away from their present location?

Francesca hadn't waited for him. She'd had the door open and was striding briskly across the lawn.

She was beautiful. Even bloody and ragged, Francesca Brown radiated with a soul-deep kind of beauty.

He shook the random thought away. He needed caffeine. Somewhere, there was a cold Mountain Dew with his name on it.

A small blur darted out from the bushes and crashed into Francesca. By the time he'd reached them, she'd picked Joey up regardless of her injury and stitches and was walking toward the back entrance, rubbing soothing circles on the child's back.

Tanner moved behind them as a shield, constantly scanning the area.

They were fifteen feet away from the door when someone yelled, "Get down!"

He leaped forward and dragged Francesca and her burden down. The bullet missed them. Barely.

This killer was becoming either bold or desperate. Neither was good.

ELEVEN

Fran clenched Joey to her chest as Tanner shielded them with his body. They child whimpered in her arms but never let go.

Officers of various ranks streamed from the building and took aim at the active sniper. They wouldn't shoot if they didn't have a clear shot. Too many civilians could be in the area. But she knew within moments the entire block would be closed off.

"Let's go." Tanner's breath fanned against her ear. He helped her stand, continuing to wedge himself between her and the sniper. No more shots broke the morning quiet. Had they got him? Or had the sniper managed to escape yet again? She didn't know how much longer she could do this and keep her equilibrium.

She held her breath until they were inside the station. The chief met them and motioned for them to go to the conference room. The smell of fresh coffee slammed into her. Her nose twitched. She normally preferred tea, but on a day like today, she'd gladly accept coffee instead.

"The sniper has been taken out," they were informed bluntly as Chief Spencer shut the door behind them. "We're running him through the system now. If we are fortunate, he'll be the sole assailant and life can return to normal."

"He won't be." Tanner spoke up. "When Francesca's place was searched earlier, we found evidence that at least two people had been there. Two sets of footprints in the dirt behind the house."

Her heart sank. "Did the sniper have a tattoo? A dragon or a sea serpent? Some kind of large red beast on his arm?"

"I can't answer that yet. What does it look like?"

Fran didn't answer. In the absence of her sketchpad, she gathered some paper from the copier and set it on the table. She started to draw the tattoo. It was a pretty vague outline.

"Joey, can you help me?"

The child's eyes were riveted to her paper. When she held out the pencil, he latched on to it. His tongue poked between his teeth. He sketched with amazing speed and accuracy, especially for one with zero training. It was all raw talent.

At first, it seemed like random doodles. He'd make a circular pattern in one corner then a scaly spike in the opposite one. For a couple of moments, it all looked like individual shapes. Then he began to connect them, and a terrifying winged dragon spread across the page, smoke curling from its flared nostrils.

She didn't question the verity of the likeness. The instant she saw it, she could imagine it on the arm of the man who'd stabbed her. It chilled her from the inside out. She rubbed her throat.

"That's it," she breathed. "That's the tattoo."

"Not only that. It's also this." Tanner showed her an image on his phone. She sucked in a breath. She'd forgotten about what he'd seen in the window. The man at the house where the Amish girl and the yet-unidentified body had been found. Somehow the attacks on her and those murders were connected.

In her gut, she wondered if Sean had been a part of what was going on. She hated to think it. But what else was she to think with Jared showing up on her lawn as this all started?

"How do Joey and Jared Murray fit into all this?" Chief Spencer wondered, echoing her own thoughts. He strolled over to the large whiteboard near the front of the room. Pictures of Jared, his mother and father, and an image she'd drawn of Joey were all there, as well as with the key information they'd gathered along the way. She needed to her sketchpad to do that drawing of the Amish girl and show it to Joey.

Tanner shook his head. "I don't know yet. But I feel like we're getting very close."

Fran didn't argue but she silently disagreed. In her opinion, they were missing some major pieces to the puzzle. The clues appeared to be random acts of violence, similar to how Joey's drawing had begun as disjointed shapes scattered over a blank page. It was only when he'd begun connecting them that a discernable form had appeared. They had a plethora of unconnected bits floating around. Now they needed to see how all the threads fit together to make sense of the motives behind the violence and lead them to arrests.

She held her thoughts to herself. She'd never been involved in this part of an investigation. Normally, she'd craft her sketches and, once the witness approved them, she'd move on to the next profile. She had always been a fan of crime shows and forensics. Being on this end of the crimes, though, was less than appealing.

Tanner's stomach growled.

"Hungry?" she asked, raising her eyebrows.

"You know it. I haven't eaten since yesterday."

She ducked her head at the reminder of his impromptu visit to the ER.

Tanner touched her cheek. The warmth of his fingertips on her skin shocked her. Her head whipped up. She stared into his eyes. "Don't you dare feel bad, Francesca. You've done nothing wrong. A little hunger won't hurt me. I'd do it again if it kept you and Joey safe."

He removed his hand. Her sensitive skin continued to tingle.

Chief Spencer cleared his throat. Francesca flushed. She'd forgotten that the chief and Joey were in the small conference room with them.

"I'm having breakfast brought in. Then we can gather and figure out the next step." The chief rose from the table and slipped from the room, closing the door behind him.

An awkward silence filled the room. Fran avoided Tanner's gaze, confused by her explosive response to his spontaneous touch. He hadn't meant anything by it. How could he? They'd only just met again after several years. The time they had spent together in the past two days had been one disaster after another. Certainly nothing conducive to kindling any romantic emotions. Yet she couldn't deny that she was attracted to him.

How had that happened?

She couldn't let it continue, of course. Not only did he live several hours away, but she'd endured all the rejection and disappointment in relationships she was ever going to put herself through. He'd be better off moving on then setting his sights on someone like her. She was alone, and she liked it that way.

Didn't she?

Shaking off the question, she moved closer to Joey. He

didn't acknowledge her, wrapped up in his drawing. She glanced idly at it. Her eyes shot wide open.

"Tanner!"

He bounced up from his seat and rushed over, standing so close she could feel his body heat. She kept her attention riveted to the sheet of paper on the table in front of them. "Look at what he's drawn."

Tanner's stare left her face and dropped to the sketch in question. She knew the moment he realized what he was seeing by his rough inhalation.

"Is that…?"

"It is. In perfect detail."

Joey had recreated the image of the young Amish girl they'd found yesterday. Fran's chest ached. The sweet face laughed up at them, her eyes open wide. It was only a pencil sketch, but joy leaped from the page.

Did he know the girl he'd drawn was dead? They had no way of knowing how much he understood.

He finished that drawing and began a second face. By the time the chief ushered in Sergeant Beck and Officer McCoy with some food, two more faces had been added to the page. That of an older man and a woman.

Steve and Tanner held a quiet conference in the corner of the room. Steve nodded and approached the table where they sat.

"Joey," he murmured softly. He reached over and touched the face of the girl. *"Wer ist das?"*

Fran blinked. She'd never considered that Steve might have learned some Pennsylvania Dutch since marrying his formerly Amish wife.

Joey smiled and patted the girl's face. "Mitty." He muttered something else too fast for Fran to catch.

"What did he say?"

"He said that is Mitty, his sister."

His sister? Oh, their poor parents!

"What about the other two?" Although she suspected they were the faces most dear to him, those of his parents.

Steve pointed to each picture.

"Mamm. Daed."

"Mom and Dad."

The chief strode to the table. "Let's make copies of these. We don't have much, but we have the likeness of his folks. Maybe it will be enough."

Fran hoped so. Part of her was relieved to finally have a name for the dead girl. No one should be forgotten. They still didn't know the identity of the other dead body, but her intuition told her they'd found the final resting place of Darcy Murray. Now they had to prove it.

Tanner could not remove his eyes from the three faces drawn on the pristine white paper. The sight of them sent chills racing down his spine, particularly the face of the girl. He'd seen her, cold and dead, less than a day ago. Seeing her so alive and happy brought the tragedy home to him.

It also reminded him how short and uncertain life was.

His own brother had stood toe to toe with his mortality and, while bruised and haunted, had retained an unshakeable faith.

Tanner's faith seemed so small in comparison. Francesca had dealt with so much more, and yet he knew she hadn't failed to cling to her beliefs when the storms blew in.

If he'd suffered what she had, or what his brother had, would he have run for cover and left his faith behind, or would he have stood strong?

He focused on Joey. The kid had a rare gift even though he was barely more than a toddler. The boy was a prodigy.

His untutored hands had recreated virtual lifelike images of those he knew and loved best.

Tanner had promised to keep them safe. He needed a plan on how to do that. Because. obviously, the threats wouldn't stop until someone died or was thrown in an iron cage. He preferred the last option.

An officer came to the door and requested the chief's presence. Tanner watched the two men move out in the hall. He could see their conversation through the window, although he couldn't hear it. The chief's expression became increasingly tight the longer they talked. Whatever it was, it wasn't good.

Then again, what about this whole case had been good?

He sent a sidelong glance at Fran and surprised her watching him. She turned away after a moment, but he'd seen the new awareness in her gaze. And the guarded way she held herself. She didn't want this attraction any more than he did. He didn't have the time for emotional entanglements.

Nor would she want anything to do with him after he gave her the news he'd been withholding. He'd meant to tell her about Sean's dealings the moment he'd seen her this morning, but that had quickly gone awry.

His stomach growled again. Pushing away his morose thoughts, Tanner helped himself to a cinnamon-raisin bagel and spread a thick layer of plain cream cheese on each slice. In general, he avoided carb-heavy foods such as bagels. This morning, though, he made an exception without guilt. As an afterthought, he took a spoonful of fruit and poured it next to the bagel. Swiping the Mountain Dew he'd been drinking from the table, he moved closer to Francesca and sat down. Only after he sat did he recall his plan to avoid her.

The chief reentered the room. Officer McCoy offered him a cup of coffee. He held up his hand and politely declined. When he was sure he had everyone's attention, he began to speak.

"I want to give you an update on our progress so far." The room was so quiet, his low voice easily carried. "The sniper shot off the roof this morning has been identified as Leo Ivans, a known mercenary who accepts hit contracts. We don't know who hired him yet. We are still searching for another man. One with this tattoo."

The chief pinned the picture of the tattoo on the board. Next to the tattoo, he pinned a copy of the picture Joey had drawn. "This girl is Mitty. Pretty sure that's not her full name. We don't know why she was taken or when. She and Joey were probably taken together. She was his sister. We're not sure what district. We are still searching for where they're from."

He pointed to a photo of Darcy Murray, one that had been printed from the DMV register. "As most of you know, this is Darcy Murray."

"Darcy. Darcy," Joey began to chant.

"She was the wife of Judge Murray."

Tanner's gut clenched when the chief used the word *was*. Chief Spencer was always careful to be correct. The word choice was no accident. He knew what he'd hear before the chief said it.

"To my sorrow, I was informed five minutes ago that the body found along with Mitty's yesterday was indeed Mrs. Murray. She disappeared several months ago. Less than a month later, Jared, her son, disappeared from protective custody. We don't know if he knew his mother's fate or if he left to find her. The coroner called me personally to inform me that he'd identified the second body as Darcy Murray."

Francesca half raised her hand. "Sir? Can I ask how? There's been no time to do a DNA analysis. And she wasn't recognizable."

"All true. However, Darcy had been in a car accident several years back. She'd suffer multiple injuries and breaks which required several pins and a plate. The coroner was able to match the numbers of these with her charts. It's her."

No one spoke. The atmosphere grew thick.

After a moment, the chief continued. "Also, we believe the same people responsible for these deaths were responsible for Jared's murder and for the attacks on our own Fran Brown, Lieutenant Kathy Bartlett, Officer Josh Lucas and Special Agent Tanner Hall."

Tanner's jaw dropped before he caught himself. He hadn't realized the team here had come to view him as part of them. Maybe it was a temporary part, but he was honored nonetheless.

Francesca reached down and discreetly squeezed his hand. He returned the gesture. To his surprise, she didn't remove the hand. Warmth flooded him at the simple show of solidarity. Her touch meant more to him than he was able, or willing, to explain.

"Children Services is asking for additional protection while they care for Joey—"

Francesca scooted her chair back and stood. "No, sir."

The room officers in the room startled. All heads whipped to stare at her. She kept her gaze trained on the chief. Tanner felt her tremble. Standing up and disagreeing with the man she respected wasn't easy for her. Admiration burst inside him.

Francesca Brown was a woman without equal.

TWELVE

Fran clasped her hands together behind her back to hide the way they trembled. She had never openly disagreed with any chief of police. Not publicly. If she held a dissenting opinion, she always went to them privately. It was her way of showing her respect for the badge. It was also how she supported the team.

She couldn't do that. Not this time. She'd let them convince her to send Joey with a social worker before. That had nearly ended with catastrophic results. Never one to make waves, she'd willingly cause a tsunami of dissent to protect the little boy who'd wormed his way into her heart.

"Fran? Please feel free to speak." Chief Spencer smiled at her. His tone rang with sincerity. She thought she caught a twinkle of approval, too, but must have been mistaken. She was publicly rejecting his directive.

"Yes, sir. Sorry, sir. The last time he was left with them, he escaped and came looking for me. The only way to stop that from happening is to keep him with me. I'll stay here, or anywhere you need me to be, but I must insist that I stay with Joey while the search for his family continues." She raised her chin and waited for his response.

"Sean's boat," Tanner said beside her.

She furrowed her brow and stared down at him. "Huh?"

"I still have the keys to Sean's boat in the marina. He never had time for it, so our bargain was that as long as I maintained it, I had unlimited access to it. We can take it out and hide in it. Who'd expect us to be in a boat?"

She thought about it. She'd forgotten about the boat, but it would serve for a short time. They could have privacy and not worry about cars approaching. There would be no neighbors. "It might work for a day or two while the investigation continues."

"Fine," Chief Spencer declared. She stared at him, openmouthed. "You never let me finish, Fran. I was going to say that while they wanted more protection, social services hadn't worked the first time, and I wanted to keep the team focused. Having Agent Hall look after you and our young friend fits my plan perfectly."

She flushed. She'd completely jumped the gun. But she was more pleased than embarrassed. The chief had agreed and hadn't been irritated by her forcefulness. Confrontation wasn't something she enjoyed, and she doubted she'd make a habit of it, but it felt good to have her opinion validated.

"One thing, Fran. I need a sketch of Joey. We'll start canvassing the local districts today and work our way out. Lieutenant Bartlett will be joining us."

"Sir!"

"Sergeant Beck?"

"Joss can take copies of the image to her parents' bishop. Also, she can contact her brothers. They can help."

Fran nodded. Joss was not only a wonderful friend, she also came with useful contacts. Her oldest brother, Micah, was a deputy US marshal. Her brother Isaiah was a former bounty hunter. The Bender men knew how to get answers.

"Great idea. Officer Yates will remain on deck here as

our coordinator with the other precincts. Agent Hall, what's the status of your vehicle?"

"I had a text about an hour ago. A new SUV will be delivered here within the hour. Then Francesca, Joey and I can head out. We'll keep in touch via cell phone. Call-ins on a regular schedule."

"Perfect. Let's do this."

The team dispersed. Fran asked Officer McCoy to get her some more paper and pencils. Once she had the supplies in hand, she sat across from Joey and sketched his likeness while he ate with single-minded attention. She completed the drawing and handed it to Officer Andrew Yates when he entered the room.

The young officer flashed her a youthful grin and tossed a salute. "This is what I was after. I'll get this out ASAP."

She grinned at his energetic manner then turn back to Joey. A laugh escaped her. Joey had pushed his plate aside, laid his head on the table and was fast asleep.

"Looks like we're not the only ones who've had a rough night." She nudged Tanner with her elbow. "Poor kid's worn out."

Tanner glanced at the sleeping child.

The breath caught in her throat at the tenderness on his face. In her mind, she envisioned him surrounded by children. It was easy to see him in the role of favorite uncle. Or father. She tore her mind away from the image. She had no business thinking of him in such a personal way.

"He's been a trouper," Tanner murmured, totally unaware of her thoughts. "I know all this must be difficult for him. It's so far from what his normal routine would be. But he hasn't protested as much as I would expect."

She scoffed slightly. "Other than leading the police and Children Services on an early morning goose chase."

He chuckled. "Yeah. I kinda forgot about that."

His expression sobered. "Once we get my new vehicle and leave, I need to talk to you."

Her chest tightened. She'd forgotten. He'd found the box Sean had hidden. Judging from his expression, it couldn't have been good news. Oh, why had she told him where it was? She forced herself to breathe slowly. She'd done the right thing; she knew she had. If Sean had been into something illegal, her hiding evidence wouldn't help. She couldn't go against her principles. Not even for the memory of the husband she'd loved.

She nodded at him then dropped her eyes. She didn't trust herself to speak at the moment. His hand touched hers.

"I know this is hard, but you'll get through it."

He couldn't promise that. No one knew what challenges, or who, they'd confront at the next bend in the road. All they could do is stay the course and trust God to guide them.

He wished he hadn't mentioned the subject of Sean's secret. The joy on her face the seconds before, when she'd laughed with him, had brought a slight lump to his throat. At that moment, he'd completely understood what it meant to want what he could never have.

He wanted Francesca Brown at his side. Not for a day. Not for a year. But for the rest of his life. He wanted to do the impossible and raise a family with her. It was so easy to imagine her exerting her subtle control over a group of rowdy Hall children. What would it be like to watch the changes in her as the years passed? To have the honor of seeing the first strands of silver appear in her hair while his own shocking red faded like his mother's. Or to hold hands as they walked?

All of these thoughts collided inside, causing an avalanche of longing. But he couldn't have what he wanted. He was too damaged. He tried not to think of it but, physically, he looked fine, until he removed his shirt. His back and one arm were scarred from burns in an explosion a few years ago. He didn't want to think of those glorious amber eyes turning dark with revulsion.

He'd been devastated by Amber's rejection. He'd been so sure that their relationship had the potential to be something strong and beautiful. It had only taken her an hour to disabuse him of that notion.

He'd brought up the box in a rush of self-preservation. And the moment he had, regret rolled through him. He couldn't take the words back. Maybe it was better this way. After all, he had seen very little indication that she felt the same way.

She had squeezed his hand. But that could be general support or sympathy.

"Agent Hall?" Officer Yates stuck his head back through the door. "Your chariot has arrived."

He grinned at the kid. He couldn't help it. Enthusiasm oozed from his pores.

Fran snickered. "What a ham."

"Yeah. But I like his energy."

"True."

Tanner stood and walked around the other side of the table. With the care he'd use if he were to pick up a sleeping cobra, he slid his arms around Joey and lifted him. His shoulder protested. Between his scarred back and arm, the bruised ribs and his aching shoulder, he was a mess.

He followed Officer Yates out of the station, hearing Francesca's light steps echoing behind him. At the SUV, he was surprised to find a booster seat had already been installed. He quirked his eyebrow and looked at Officer Yates.

"The chief had us grab one while we were getting the food this morning."

"So, he planned for us to take him all along," Francesca mused. "My burst of defiance served no purpose."

"It was great! You were bold and confident. One has to admire a woman who stands up for herself and others."

She laughed lightly. "Thanks. I don't think it'll happen often. I used all my defiance on my parents."

She'd said her folks had abandoned her for not going along with their wishes. In his mind, they'd lost more than she had that day. He could almost feel sorry for them. If he weren't so aggravated on her behalf. It was wrong, the way they'd turned their backs on her.

"Please, God, don't let him wake up," he muttered as he crawled into the back seat and placed Joey in the booster seat.

"Amen," Francesca said fervently.

To his amazement, Joey never stirred. He backed out and shut the door. "Why don't you ride in front this time? If we need to adjust later, we will. But we can talk quieter if we both sit in the front."

She nodded and climbed into the front passenger seat. "Can we go by my house for a few minutes? I don't want to travel in my pajamas."

He wanted to say no, but her house was on the way.

"Can you keep it to under ten minutes?"

"Yes."

He nodded and called Steve to give him a heads-up. "I don't want to leave Joey unattended in the car, nor do I want Francesca alone in the house."

"Melissa and I are heading out. We'll meet you there."

He happened to look up in time to see Francesca roll her eyes. "Hey. None of that. You might think it's overkill, but your safety is on my shoulders."

"I know. I'm not complaining."

"Not out loud. But I heard your eyes rolling."

"Please." She bit her lip. "So, tell me about the box."

He wanted to wait, but they may only have minutes before Joey woke up. "As you probably know, it was an account under Sean's name in an out-of-state bank. The deposits stopped two months before his death. We haven't located the account they came from yet. I think it was closed out."

"Was he embezzling?"

He shrugged, uncomfortable with the conversation. "That or doing some sort of illegal service. Maybe even bribery. What we do know, and this is interesting, is even though the money was put into the account, he never took a single cent out."

She was silent for half a minute. "What does that mean?"

"Not sure. But we're still looking at all angles. It's also evident you never touched it, nor was your name attached to it."

Her head jerked back. "I had nothing to do with it."

"I know. But my boss confirmed that."

She firmed her lips, a sure sign she was annoyed, but didn't say anything more. He let her stew the rest of the trip, knowing she needed to work it out in her head. She'd brought this to him. He was only doing his job.

It felt like a lonely ride, though.

It was silly to be mad at Tanner for making sure she was in the clear. She knew it. It aggravated her that there'd been a need to clear her, though. She'd been a law-abiding citizen all her life and one stupid move from her husband had jeopardized the reputation she had painstakingly built.

Steve and Melissa followed the SUV up the driveway.

Tanner parked the vehicle near the front porch but didn't get out.

"Francesca—"

"I'm sorry," she interrupted him. "You were only doing your job. I know that. This whole situation, everything that's happened, has me tense and overreacting."

"Understandable."

Steve tapped on her window. She pushed the button on her armrest to open it.

"Listen, I'm going to do a thorough search through the house first. You don't step a foot outside this vehicle until I give the all-clear."

He didn't wait for her to respond.

She gripped her hands in her lap and waited. Finally, Melissa joined her. "When it's clear, I'm going in with you."

Fran waited until Steve came out and told her the house was clear. Then she stepped out of the vehicle and went in with Melissa. After everything that had happened, she was glad to have the other woman's company. She threw stuff into a bag without any thought of neatness.

"Make sure you have stuff for different temps. Sometimes it's a little cooler on the water."

She nodded at Melissa and gathered a sweater to add to the growing pile. Had Sean bought the boat honestly? She'd never questioned it before. Now she wondered about everything.

That was a rabbit hole she couldn't afford to go down.

"Done." She zipped her bag and they left the house.

Would she feel safe returning to this place alone? She might if she installed a security system. And got a dog.

She'd worry about that later. Right now, she had a boat to catch.

THIRTEEN

Joey awoke on the way to the boat and began to yell. He only calmed down when Tanner stopped the vehicle and Francesca slid into the back seat. She'd changed into a blouse with butterflies all over it. He'd smiled when he'd seen the way the wings of the insects glittered. She did like sparkly things.

She began to count the butterflies and soon Joey counted with her. They continued to count until they reached the marina. They'd get to twenty-five and start over. That must have been how many were on her blouse. Tanner had stopped listening after they'd started the third time. He'd be counting in his sleep.

It was a relief when they arrived at the quay.

"Is this going to bother you?" she asked while getting Joey out of the SUV.

He hefted the bag in his hand and turned to look at her, confused. "Is what going to bother me?"

"Being on a boat. It's not steady. I noticed you didn't care for the motion when we were in the car. If it would be easier on you, we could continue trying to find a safe place. One on land."

"Ah. Our nesting incident."

She rolled her eyes. She sure was cute when she was exasperated.

"No. I enjoy boating. I don't like rickety surfaces. I had a run-in with a very old bridge once and it won. Never again. And the reason the chief liked the boat idea was that it would give both of us at least a night to recuperate. Sure, we could take my car and drive to find a safe location. We probably will tomorrow. But we need to be somewhere we can rest for a few hours. A place Joey won't escape from if we both fall asleep. Sutter Springs has very few places we can hide in plain sight."

A few minutes later, they reached the boat. He went on board first and dropped off their bags. He appreciated that Steve had gathered his things from the hotel Tanner had been staying at and put them in the SUV for him.

Going back for Fran, he assisted them in climbing onto the boat. It took a few minutes to get the hang of balancing on the deck as the craft gently swayed with the motion of the water. He hadn't been lying when he'd told Fran he didn't mind the motion of the water. Even if he fell in, he'd probably not break anything or have anything crash on top of him. And the height from the deck to the water was negligible.

"You two go on down below. I'm going to start her up and move away from the dock."

Anyone who wanted them would have to use a boat or swim a mile to get to them.

There was something soothing about being on the water, he reflected five minutes later. He'd driven the boat to a secluded area, hidden from the main beach. The water was clear and there were only a few boats on the water. If it were a weekend, that would be a different story.

He wandered down the steps to check on the other two passengers. Francesca had found a sketchpad and Joey was doodling away. It wouldn't last, but for now, he was content.

"Why don't you lie down for a few minutes?" she suggested. "I'll wake you if anything happens."

He would have argued if he hadn't been swaying on his feet. This might be the only chance he'd get to rest for a while. He took advantage of it and stretched himself out on a bed in the back room.

It might have been two minutes or two hours when Francesca shook him awake. "Hey. Something's wrong."

He listened. A loud motor buzzed toward them. Swinging his legs over the edge of the bed, he ran up to the top deck and watched a small motorboat swing past them. He had a three-second view of a man's profile before his arm launched something at their boat.

A grenade!

It clattered into the hole where the anchor should have been. But the rope had been sliced. He heard the explosive roll in and clank to the bottom of the boat. It would be impossible to get it out before the entire craft was blown to smithereens.

The smaller boat revved its engine and sped away. He rushed down the stairs.

"Francesca! We have to jump ship now!"

Francesca grabbed the little boy. He screamed and fought her hold, but she held on. If she let go, he'd die. Tanner would see him home to his mama if it killed him. And at this rate, it just might.

"Life vests!" Francesca gasped out.

"There's no time." Tanner wished there was a way to ease them into the water, but they didn't have the time. "You're going to have to jump. There's a live grenade. I can't get to it. It's gonna blow any second."

The color leached from her face. She didn't complain.

"Hold your breath, Joey." She gently pressed the child's face to her shoulder and leaped. Tanner dove after them.

Joey screamed all the way down and hit the water with a splash. He came up sputtering. It took him a few seconds to get his breath and begin wailing again. But he was alive.

"Swim!"

He wanted to take Joey from her and ease the burden but knew the child wouldn't let him. "Float, I'll drag you."

She turned to her back, keeping Joey's head above the surface. Tanner grabbed her collar and kicked off, putting as much distance as possible between them and the doomed boat. He made it twenty feet away. Then thirty. He was close to fifty feet away when a *boom* thundered and the water bubbled around them. Debris rained down. Burning slivers of wood hit the water with a loud hiss before the flames were extinguished.

Tanner fought against the onslaught of bad memories and kneejerk reactions. He had to get them out of the water and to safety. Nothing else mattered.

Tanner was struggling. Fran didn't know what was going on with him, but she knew the look of trauma when she saw it. He was in a bad headspace.

Fran kept a tight hold on Joey. He'd stopped screaming, but only because the water kept getting into his mouth. He'd gag and spit it out. Tears continued to trek down his little face. She had to get both him and Tanner out of the water and on dry land soon.

And she needed to drag Tanner out of the funk he'd sunk into.

"How did they know to attack the boat?" she asked him, doing her best to keep afloat with Joey fighting her every inch.

"Huh? Um, I don't know. I never even mentioned it until this morning."

Wait a minute.

"I did."

"At the meeting."

"No. At my house. I was talking to Melissa, and we referred to my being on the water. If anyone knew Sean had a boat, it would have been an easy leap."

The bleakness faded from his expression. "There's a listening device in your home."

"Has to be."

They made it to land, shivering and chilled to the bone. The sun was high in the sky. She'd listened to the weather report yesterday while they'd been in the car. Today was supposed to be in the high eighties. If they could stay in the sunny areas, they'd have a better chance of drying out quickly and getting warm again.

"Where are we?" She glanced around. When Tanner reached for Joey, surprisingly, the small boy didn't protest. It had been a rough day. "This doesn't look anything like where we started this morning."

"Because it's not. I moved us away. We have a couple of miles to walk before we get to the car."

If the vehicle was still there.

"I'll have to check the car before you can get in," he told her, proving that, once again, they were on the same wavelength.

"Do you hear that?"

She listened. It was the sound of a motorboat. The killer was returning to the scene of the crime.

"He's probably checking to see if we are dead. We need to move."

Fran didn't have to be told twice. He increased his pace. It took two of her strides to match his, but she didn't question him. They didn't know how much time they had before the killer realized there were no bodies in the water. She panted a little at the pace. When this was over, she was renewing her gym membership.

Tanner grunted.

Guilt smote her. He had to be in pain. "Let me carry him for a few minutes. Give your shoulder a rest." He didn't argue. When he handed Joey to her, she caught a brief glimpse of thick scar tissue on the upper biceps of his right arm.

"That was from my SUV exploding several years ago," he said, his mouth smiling with a bitter twist. "I'm afraid I'm not as pretty as I used to be."

She scoffed. "And they say women are vain. Scars or not, you are probably the bravest man I know. And that's what the scars say. Nothing else."

She was a little embarrassed by her outburst, but forced herself to meet his eyes. He needed to know she didn't judge him by something so superficial. He might make fun of his scar, but it was obvious it bothered him. Someone had probably made a tasteless joke or insulted him. Maybe some woman had treated him poorly. If she ever met the woman, she'd be tempted to tell her a thing or two about Tanner Hall. Then she laughed to herself. She was ready to fight with a woman who might be a figment of her imagination.

"What's so funny?"

"Nothing. I think I'm stressed and overtired."

"Here. Switch back. I hear something coming."

Sure enough, there were steps crashing behind them. They moved faster. Fran pressed a hand against her side, trying to ease the sharp pain she'd developed there.

They reached a main road. By this time, she was limping. She didn't know how much further she could go.

FOURTEEN

Francesca was about done in. If he could wish for anything, he would wish for both her and Joey to be home safe and that all the criminals chasing them would be locked away for life in a prison cell far away. They were still at least a mile from his SUV. They were all fading fast. His shoulder was on fire. Joey didn't weigh much, but his weight, coupled with his restless writhing, created a constant pressure on the injured tissue. Every so often, Joey would kick out, jamming his small shoe directly into Tanner's bruised ribs.

He'd be absolutely useless to help anyone before this adventure ended.

He whispered a silent prayer. *Lord, please give me Your strength so I can get these two to safety.* Each prayer he said came easier than the last.

"Down. Down. Down," Joey began to chant.

"We can't put him down!" Francesca exclaimed, panic edging into her voice. "We don't know how far behind us they are!"

He tightened his hold. "Hey, buddy. We need to keep going. Okay?" He shifted the squirming child in his arms. Joey's cries grew louder. If they didn't do something, he'd have a full-blown meltdown.

"Try counting." Francesca advised.

"Counting what?"

"Anything!"

He shifted him again, then pointed to the farm at his left. "Look, Joey. Cows. I see one cow. Two cows. Three cows."

Joey's voice quieted and his fidgeting grew less pronounced. It was working. The child gradually turned his gaze to the field. His finger pointed at each cow and he added his voice to Tanner's.

He wasn't quite sure what he'd do when they ran out of cows, but he'd figure it out when they got to that point.

"Are you okay?" Francesca puffed beside him. "Do you want me to hold him for a few minutes?"

He glared at her. "You are having enough trouble keeping up as it is. Save your breath."

Hooves clattering on the tar-and-pitch-covered road broke up what promised to be a fruitless argument. He stiffened.

"Neigh! Neigh!" Joey yelled with more animation than they had seen from him yet. They'd found the one thing he seemed to connect with on a deeper emotional level.

Horses.

This particular horse, a gorgeous paint with a shining white blaze on her nose, trotted toward them, pulling the box-shaped buggy commonly found in Ohio. The buggy was black, with a front Plexiglas shield rather than a window to protect the family from any kicked-up particles of dirt or gravel. A man in his mid-thirties with a healthy beard about two inches long sat upon the front bench. As far as Tanner could see, no one was inside the buggy.

Joey bounced in his arms. He laughed and reached toward the mare slowly approaching them. Rather than pass by, as he would have expected, the man drew back on the reins, halting the mare a foot from their position.

"Is that Joey Zook?" The slightly accented voice was tinted with shock.

"Joey! Joey!" the child yelled delightedly.

"We're sure he must be," Tanner answered. "We've been trying to find out who he belongs to. Unfortunately, we are being chased."

How much did you tell civilians? On one side, you want to inform the public. But on the other, you don't want to start anyone panicking. Plus, they were still standing in the middle of the road where it wasn't safe.

"Joey's family live about a mile from here. Their oldest daughter and Joey went missing about five months ago. Hop in. I can give you a ride."

"Really? Thanks. That would be great." Tanner helped Francesca and Joey step into the back of the buggy. He followed them. He squirmed against the seat, wedging his shoulders between the wall and the back of the buggy. It was a little tight, but they were off the road and out of sight.

"How did Joey end up with you folks?"

If there was one thing Tanner didn't care for, it was answering civilian questions. Not that he minded dealing with private citizens. It was just that when they made inquiries, they didn't always understand that he couldn't give them all the answers they desired. Parts of the investigation needed to stay private.

"There's not much I can tell you. We found him, and all we could figure out was his name was Joey. We're kind of hoping that the family will be able to give us more information."

Out of the corner of his eye, he saw Francesca shaking her head. He was puzzled at first. What was she trying to say? Then he remembered something he'd heard about the Amish communities. They were not always fans of working with English law enforcement. It was possible that telling them he was with the FBI would be the quickest way of shutting down any chance of open communication.

When he talked to Joey's father, he'd have to tell him. However, this gentleman seemed to be little more than a Good Samaritan, which meant he didn't need to be in the know.

Joey rose up on his knees and twisted around so he was facing out the back window. "Cow! Cow!"

Well, at least they were in Amish country where there were lots of farm animals for Joey to count.

"How much farther?" Francesca asked.

He understood her anxiousness. It was nerve-wracking knowing that somewhere out there the man who had just tried to murder them with a hand grenade was seeking them. He dared not sit forward in case someone drove by and saw him in the back of the buggy. Both Tanner and Francesca would stick out like a black cat in a room full of white ones.

"Not much further. Just around the next corner. Jeremiah Zook and his wife have been grieving for Joey and Amity."

"Mitty," Francesca murmured. "That must have been his way of saying Amity."

"Mitty," Joey repeated.

"What happened to her? Did you ever see her?"

"I've never talked to her," Tanner hedged. No one should know about her murder until after her parents had been informed.

"What!" the buggy driver exclaimed.

Tanner blinked at the response. Then dread filled his heart. An engine roared up behind the buggy way too fast. His instincts screamed at him to take Joey and Francesca and hide them until they were safe. He never got the chance.

"He's trying to run us off the road!"

That seemed to be a favorite tactic of his.

The horse squealed. Tanner leaned forward. The truck came at them again. He must have seen Joey in the window. If only Tanner had his phone, he could call the incident in and request backup. Unfortunately, when they'd dived into the water, his phone had also plunged into the chilly abyss. As had his gun. So not only could he not call anyone, he'd be dead in the water, so to speak, if anyone came at them with a weapon.

"He's coming back!"

The truck sped past them. For a moment, Tanner thought it was all a mistake. Until the white brake lights flashed. He was going to ram into the horse. "Watch out! He's going into Reverse!"

The truck shot backward, its spinning wheels spewing gravel and mud. Large chunks spattered against the Plexiglas windshield. The horse whinnied and tossed its head, backing up and forcing the buggy with it. The buggy driver had no control anymore. No matter how he tried to hold the reins, the horse would not settle.

There was a large ditch on the side of the road. If the buggy went into that, it would be stuck there. Tanner wasn't even sure how they would get out of the buggy since there was only a door on the one side. They would be stuck inside like sardines in a can just waiting for somebody to rip it open. He didn't plan on staying and being that vulnerable.

With an extra-loud squeal, the mare reared up, her front legs slashing the air. She continued backing up, pushing the buggy back with her rump. The rear tire went over the edge of the ditch. The buggy jolted. He wasn't sure, but Tanner thought he had felt the rear axle snap. If that happened, they weren't going to be going anywhere fast.

"What do I do?" the driver yelled.

Tanner had had enough. It was time to be bold. He slid out the door of the buggy, holding on as best he could. Francesca called out to him, her voice sharper than normal, but he ignored her. He could not lose his focus now. When his feet hit the ground, the motion of the buggy nearly pulled them out from under him. He got his balance and released the buggy. Then he launched himself at the truck. The driver had put the vehicle in Park and was messing around with something at his side.

Probably a gun.

He expected the driver to look up and attempt to run over him, but apparently, he hadn't noticed Tanner leave the buggy. That worked in Tanner's favor, so he wouldn't complain. He ran to the driver side of the truck and yanked on the handle.

The nice thing about twenty-year-old pickup trucks was that they didn't have automatic locks. The door swung open with a whiny creak. Tanner took hold of the driver's left arm and yanked him down out of the cab.

It was the guy with the dragon tattoo. Tanner heard Joey's shrill cry. He'd recognized the man too.

Tanner was exhausted, with too many injuries to numerate. But the sound of Joey's anguish reminded him of all the horror and sadness people he cared about had suffered for the past few days because of this man. Fury filled him with strength, allowing him to overpower the man. During the scuffle, the attacker smashed his head against a rock and knocked himself unconscious, giving Tanner the opportunity to bind his hands with rope from the buggy.

Now what to do with him?

"There's a community phone booth right beyond the Zook place," the buggy driver offered. "Call for help. I'll wait here. I can't drive my buggy until it's repaired. When you see Jeremiah, tell him my troubles. He'll know what to do."

"We'll have to walk," Francesca murmured to Tanner.

He nodded. "I would hate to contaminate any evidence in that truck."

Tanner and Francesca held Joey's hands between them and walked in the direction the man had pointed. He was so weary, it felt like he was walking through sand. Every step was an effort. It wasn't until they had turned onto the Zook's road that Tanner realized It he'd never gotten the man's name. It just showed how exhausted he was. Basic communication skills had gone down the drain.

But they were about to reintroduce Joey to his family. The joy mingled with the sorrow that they'd also have to tell them about Amity. There was never a good way to tell a family a child had been wrongfully murdered.

Then they began walking up the path to the front door.

Joey recognized where they were and began yelling. Within seconds, a woman ran out the door, calling for her husband. She flew down the steps and engulfed Joey in a tearful embrace.

"Did she suffer?"

Parents always wanted to know that. Fran wanted to say no, but she didn't know how Amity died. She looked helplessly at Tanner.

"No, Mrs. Zook. I talked with the coroner yesterday. Your daughter didn't suffer."

Laura Zook mopped her cheeks with the dishtowel that had been on the countertop when they'd arrived twenty minutes earlier. She'd shooed the other children outside to play while the adults talked. They hadn't gotten much further than telling her how they'd found Joey and the discovery of Amity.

Jeremiah Zook had stalked out ten minutes ago. He'd claimed he was off to assist the neighbor who'd helped them. Fran strongly suspected he'd needed a few moments to grieve in private. She absolutely understood such a need, having felt the same way after Sean died.

"It was that boy," Laura moaned.

"What boy?" Fran held her breath. She had a feeling things were going to start to make sense.

"Amity hadn't joined the church yet. It was her time of choosing. She had started driving around with an *Englisch* boy. Jared. I don't remember his last name. I didn't want her to, but it is our way not to interfere so our *kinder* can make their own decisions. It does no *gut* to join the church if it was forced. Better to leave than to promise your life to *Gott* and not mean it."

Fran nodded to show she understood.

"Amity told us she was leaving with her young man. We hoped she'd *cumme* home someday. We weren't worried until the next day when we couldn't find Joey." She patted the child as if to reassure herself that he was still there.

"How do you think he ended up with them?" Fran asked softly.

"*Ach.* I know what happened. Joey was fascinated with Jared's car. He would climb in it and hide all the time."

Fran's heart stuttered at the name. Amity and Jared had been in love. Had Jared been trying to return Joey?

Tanner excused himself and stepped out to use the community phone booth to contact the chief to tell him to send someone for tattoo guy. He'd also told him what they'd learned of the connection between Amity and Jared. When he returned, he whispered to her that Amity had been dead several days before Jared. What had happened?

"Someone's taking our attacker into custody. And Steve's coming to get us."

She nodded, keeping her attention on Joey's mother.

"Did that young man kill my daughter?"

She shook her head. "No, ma'am. He was murdered as well. We don't know by who or why yet."

Jeremiah entered, his face stoic. Only his swollen eyes showed the truth.

There wasn't much more to add.

When Steve arrived, Tanner and Fran stood to leave. Fran squatted close to Joey. "Goodbye Joey."

He patted her cheek with his hand, although he didn't speak. She hadn't expected him to. He was home. She'd been a security blanket when he had been frightened. He no longer needed her.

She fell asleep to the motion of Steve's cruiser. When she awoke, Tanner was gone.

"Where'd he go?" She rubbed her eyes. They felt like she'd slept in a sandbox.

"I dropped him off at his car. We decided to let you sleep. You were wiped out."

So was Tanner. She knew she had no control over what he did, but he couldn't stop her from worrying about him. She closed her eyes again, although she knew she wouldn't be able to go back to sleep. It was easier than engaging in small talk. She was too raw to hold it together.

A moment later, she remembered "tattoo guy," as Tanner called him.

"Did we get him? The guy who tried to kill me?"

Steve nodded. "Pretty sure we did, yeah."

"In that case, can you drop me off at home rather than take me back to the station?"

"Let's compromise. The station is on the way. I need to grab something. You wait in the car, I'll run and grab it, then I'll drive you home. Okay?"

"Sounds fair." She nodded. "Yes, that will work. Thanks."

Fran leaned her head against the cool window and forced herself to relax. As she'd surmised, she wasn't able to fall asleep again. However, she expected that just resting her eyes would benefit her greatly. It had been a very long few days. Steve pulled into the parking lot and put the car in Park, but he left the motor running.

"I'll be right back."

She waved her hand, telling him to go. "I'll be here when you get back."

Two minutes later, someone knocked on her window. She turned and saw that, rather than Steve, it was Tanner standing outside. She rolled down her window, curious to know what he would say now that the danger had been eliminated.

Tanner leaned down and folded his forearms across the bottom of the window so that they were eye to eye. "Hey. Steve says you wanna go back to your house rather than come in and meet with the team. Are you alright?"

"I am. I just need some time to decompress. It's been an intense couple of days. How about you? You've taken quite a few hits since this started."

"Nothing that a few days off won't fix."

He opened his mouth as if to say something, closed it, and tried again. Giving up after the third attempt, he growled low in his throat and ducked his head into the window. Their noses almost touched. Then he angled his head and brushed a gentle kiss over her sensitive lips. Startled, she froze for a second. It had been a long time since she'd kissed a man. But it felt right with Tanner. Closing her lids, she allowed herself permission to kiss him back. He lifted his head and brushed a hand down her face.

Then he was gone.

Steve returned a moment later, a self-satisfied smirk hovering about his mouth. She suspected he'd seen the kiss. But since he wasn't asking, she kept quiet.

She hadn't wanted a complication like Tanner in her life. Had fought against it. But now she'd miss him when he left. Somehow, the complication she hadn't wanted was one she now craved.

FIFTEEN

Two days later, Fran was back at the station working on some sketches for a different case. She had not seen Tanner since the kiss they had exchanged the other day. She waffled back and forth about whether or not she wanted to see him. Would it be awkward? It wasn't like they were dating or a couple. They had shared a kiss.

But it had felt like a pretty life-changing kiss to her. She still found herself daydreaming about it. What if it hadn't meant anything to him?

She did know that he hadn't been around yesterday. He'd returned to the Cleveland office to report to his boss. When she'd heard that he had left, she'd been devastated that he'd gone without saying a word to her. All day yesterday, she'd been cranky, snapping at people and, in general, in a bad mood. It was all Tanner's fault. If he hadn't kissed her, she would never have felt so confused or unsettled.

Then this morning while she'd been working, she'd heard his laugh in the other room and it had suddenly felt like the clouds hanging over her dissipated. It was kind of scary that one man could affect her mood and personality to that extent.

It wasn't like she needed his protection anymore. The man with the tattoo on his arm was in prison, charged with the murders of both Amity and Darcy. Although he hadn't confessed to it, they also believed that he had murdered Jared. That meant he was also likely the one who had forced them off the cliff.

He had a lot to answer for. She shook her head. How did somebody think they had the right to take another life? Was it all about money?

The part that hurt was that she still didn't know how or if Sean played into it. She sighed and focused back in on her drawing.

Someone tapped on the window. She glanced up with a cautious smile. The moment she saw the woman standing in the door, her jaw fell open. Dropping her pencil to the table, she ignored it when it rolled off the other side.

She charged over to her sister.

"Stacy!" Fran swooped in to give her sister a hug. Stacy remained stiff in her arms. Fran tried to block the pain spiraling through her at the pointed rejection. If she wasn't there to reconcile, why had she come? No. She wouldn't assume the worst. "Where's Lucy? Why are you here?"

She'd never object to seeing her baby sister, but Stacy had all but severed their connection. Why renew it now?

Tanner glanced up in time to see Fran exit the front door of the station with another woman. The other woman held herself stiffly, keeping a solid foot between them. Despite her odd, rather cold demeanor, Tanner saw the resemblance in the high cheekbones, widow's peak and shape of the mouth. Where Fran's expression tended to fascinate him with its sheer mobility and animation, this woman's expression was so cautious, it bordered on robotic.

Even from the distance, he could see the pain emanating from Fran in silent waves. She'd been waiting for the chance to reestablish a relationship with her sister, at the very least. Well, her sister was there, but it didn't look like a reunion was what she had in mind.

He didn't pause to consider his actions before he changed course to intercept them. "Hey, Francesca," he called lightly when he stood a few feet away. "What's up?"

If she wanted his help, she'd let him know.

Briefly, her face lit up. Then she gazed at her sister and the flicker of animation disappeared. "Tanner. This is my sister, Stacy Reynolds. I don't think I need any assistance right now. We're just going somewhere to talk. I'll be back in a few minutes."

"If I don't see you in thirty, I'll send out a search party." He'd said it as a joke, but he'd wanted her to know he was there if she needed him.

She nodded gratefully then continued to walk toward the parking lot.

Frowning, he watched for about ten seconds before shaking his head. He couldn't stand around all day. He hoped to have something substantial to report by the time she returned from her chat. Maybe she'd have her sister with her, and they could actually have a conversation. He'd be nice, but he wanted to be sure Stacy knew that hurting Francesca again was not acceptable.

He shrugged and opened the door to enter the building.

"Hey, Tanner. You're going to want to join us." Steve waved him into the conference room.

He cast one last glance at the door Francesca's retreating back before joining the chief and the other officers.

Fifteen minutes later, the acid in his stomach roiled. SAC Mitchell called to announce that Judge Murray had been found murdered in his cell. They'd always suspected that someone else had been working with the judge, selling weapons illegally. The judge had finally agreed to share information in return for a shorter sentence.

He never got the chance.

Even worse, Francesca remained in danger. The man in jail for Amity's and Darcy's murders had been a hired killer named Darren Dutcliff. Darren had also killed Sean. And during his intake, he'd sneered that he wouldn't be the last one to come after "that little sneak's wife."

Sean.

Sean hadn't been dirty, Tanner had been relieved to learn. He'd been building a case, trying to take down part of the ring himself. But why? Why wouldn't he have gone to Tanner or SAC Mitchell?

It reeked of a personal vendetta. But why, Tanner couldn't say. All he knew was that the judge had had someone on the outside leading his agenda.

And now the judge himself was dead. The working theory was that whoever he'd been in cahoots with had acted to shut him up—permanently.

They were still discussing this when Officer Yates dashed through the door. "New information!" he announced. "One of Jared's old school friends received a letter. Jared told him that if he didn't contact him in six days, to open it and read it."

They all waited.

Finally, the chief demanded, "Well? Did he?"

"Yes. Darren Dutcliff had tracked Jared down after he left WITSEC. Jared had watched Darren Dutcliff murder his girlfriend when she entered his home at the wrong time, interrupting an attempt on Jared's life. What we didn't know was that he'd also seen someone else murder his mother. He didn't know who it was, but his mother had told him that Sean Brown had come to talk to her six years ago. He thought he knew the identity of someone high up in the ring and was trying to frame them by posing as a dirty agent. When Jared saw his mother murdered, he knew it was the ringleader, but he didn't know who it was. He and Amity knew Jared was in danger. They'd suspected he was being followed. They planned on bringing Joey home once the danger was over. Amity didn't want to endanger her parents. She was afraid they'd get hurt, or that they'd blame Jared."

Tanner thought about it. "I think he probably took Joey to Francesca's, hoping that as Sean's widow and working with the police, she'd be able to return Joey to his home. Then he was killed before he could contact her." His stomach curdled. "Did he say anything about the identity of the man?"

"Here's the letter that he sent. There's a picture in there, too, although I'm not clear why."

Tanner took the letter and read through it. Nothing new. Then he turned over the picture. It was a wedding photo. "Hey. Here's Darcy." He pointed her out in the background.

"I don't recognize the couple," Steve said.

Tanner looked at the groom. Never seen him before. Then he looked at the bride. With a shout, he stood up. He'd seen her less than an hour ago.

"That's Stacy Reynolds, Francesca's sister. Stacy severed all contact with Fran years ago, and she never knew why. The deposits Sean made were from a CR. What is Anastasia Reynolds's husband's name?"

Steve was already online. "Chad. Chad Reynolds."

Tanner ran for the door. "He's going to try and kill Francesca if he knows she found what her husband had done."

Stacy glanced around Fran's yard. Instead of the distain Fran had expected, she saw longing and a depth of sadness that shocked her. She wanted to wrap her in a hug. But she remembered how Stacy had reacted before, so she kept her distance.

"Why are you here? You haven't talked with me in years."

Finally, Stacy faced her. "I couldn't. My husband, he was an abusive monster, although it took me a long time to realize it. When I told Mom and Dad, they told me not to shame the family by being weak. That I was married to one of the movers and shakers in our community. What did it matter if I felt a little isolated or alone? When I asked him for a divorce, he threatened to take Lucy from me."

She covered her mouth, but the sob broke free anyway. This time, when Fran took her in her arms, Stacy wept on her shoulder.

"Tell me what you need."

Stacy lifted her head. "I heard him. On the phone. He had it on speaker. The man on the line told him he needed to prove himself. Chad told him he had a list of people he'd killed on his command. A judge. A witness. And then... oh, Fran, Chad said he'd even killed his brother-in-law."

She had to sit down, but there wasn't a dry spot outside. White noise buzzed inside her head. "I don't understand. I've never even met your husband. Why would he want Sean dead?"

"Because he was collecting evidence against me and thought I didn't know," a man's voice answered.

Both women wheeled around. Chad Reynolds stood before them with a gun in his hand.

He flicked a scornful glance at Fran. "I don't know what information Jared was able to share with you before he was taken care of. It doesn't matter anymore. You're a loose end. Between him and that boy, you'd be able to figure out who I was. It was only a matter of time. I never expected you to be so elusive."

"I never talked with Jared!"

He shrugged. "Regardless, you know too much. Hmm. What to do? I don't want blood in my car. It will have to be here. I saw some new cameras in your house. But not in your shed."

He herded them into the shed Sean had converted to his tool shop. Fran nearly laughed with hysteria. She'd made good on her plan to install a security system and hadn't done that building because she hadn't been inside it in over six years.

"That's far enough." They stopped two feet inside the shed. He closed the door behind him. "Anastasia, you seemed like such a perfect wife when we married. I guess I was wrong."

He got too close and Stacy reached out to attack him. His thick glasses fell to the floor and crunched. But she was no match for him.

"That wasn't very smart." He aimed and squeezed the trigger.

SIXTEEN

"Stacy!" Fran caught her sister before she hit the ground. She staggered under her sister's weight. Stacy was a few inches taller than she was and at least twenty pounds heavier. But Fran was strong. After the initial surprise, she regained her balance and gently lowered her sister to the floor and knelt beside her, disregarding both the layers of dirt and crawling critters on the surface and the blood staining her once-immaculate blouse. All that mattered was her baby sister, bleeding out in her arms.

Tearing off her lightweight jacket, she pressed it over the wound on her sister's shoulder to staunch the flow. Within seconds, deep red seeped into it and covered her fingers. Desperately, she scanned the interior for anything else she could use. There was nothing.

Finally, her seething gaze settled on Chad, Stacy's no-good husband.

"You shot her!" she accused, astonished and appalled. "Why? Stacy has no part of this!"

Chad ambled forward, still holding the gun, and looked at his wife. The absolute lack of expression on his face chilled Fran clean through. Stacy's lids flickered open. Her face was bone-white, and pain cut deep lines on either side of her pinched mouth.

"He knew I'd found out," she gasped, her words breathless. "He was stealing from the judge. He'd thought Sean was helping him. When he found out Sean was playing him, he ordered his death. He was the one who controlled the judge and ordered Jared killed. And you."

"I didn't want this, Anastasia," Chad said, his calm demeanor much the same as if he were discussing something he'd seen on the news. Disconnected. "You were the perfect wife, the perfect image. But I knew you wouldn't stay quiet. I'm sure you can see my predicament. I have too much at stake to let you ruin it for me. Goodbye, my love."

He raised the gun again.

Fran knew he'd kill both of them without a single qualm. She had faith that Tanner would figure out where she was and who had been behind all the murder and mayhem. But she also knew it would take too long for him to arrive. By the time the cavalry arrived, both Stacy and she would be dead, and Chad would be on his way to a new identity and a new life.

No, if they had any chance of getting out of this alive, it was up to her to make it happen.

Fran leaned down and kissed her sister on the forehead. The cold skin alarmed her.

"I've got this," she whispered. Leaning back, she saw her sister's unflinching gaze resting on her, as if she didn't see the menace of her husband approaching. In that instance, Fran knew what her edge was. Chad had a gun, but when Stacy had attacked him, his glasses had been knocked off and crushed beneath her heel. The lenses had been thick, she recalled. He could barely make them out! That's why he'd missed before. "Hold this over the wound."

Stacy groaned but brought her uninjured arm around and placed it on the sodden clothing, keeping it in place. It might not be enough pressure, but that would be insignificant if she failed to disarm Chad in the next five seconds.

His finger was on the trigger.

Fran slipped the shoe from her foot and slung it at him. It crashed into his wrist, knocking the gun from his hand. The weapon fired, burying the bullet five inches from Stacy's head.

It was enough. Shoving off the filthy floor, Fran launched herself at her brother-in-law. He was bigger than she was, but she had the advantage of clear vision and self-defense training. When he tried to swing around and catch her from behind, she jammed an elbow into his solar plexus.

"Oof!" Chad doubled over, clutching at his stomach.

She didn't give him time to recover. Using her still-shod foot, she kicked out at his kneecap. It gave a satisfying *pop* an instant before Chad's shriek pierced her eardrums. She winced. He was on the ground, his hands grasping the injured knee as a tear fell from his eye to create a tiny drop of mud on the floor. Fran ran to the worktable and yanked open the top drawer. It had been left for so long, it was stuck. She had to pull twice, putting her back into it. Finally, it flew open. She knew her husband had kept zip ties in there among his plethora of supplies.

"Please, God. Let them be here. Aha!" Grabbing the package of extra-long ties, she charged back to Chad. He was beginning to rise. She didn't bother with any fancy moves. Just literally bowled him over. He went down, hard. His head bounced against the packed earth with a meaty thud.

When he lay there without moving, she dropped beside him and placed her fingers against the pulse on his neck. A steady thump at her fingertips convinced her he was well. That and the continuous rise of his chest. She rolled him onto his side and yanked both arms behind his back.

It took her a few moments, but she managed to get both wrists anchored together. She then went to work on his ankles. When she was satisfied that he was trussed up as securely as a lassoed bull at a rodeo, she abandoned him and rushed back to Stacy.

"Pretty slick moves, sis."

The tears she hadn't allowed herself a few minutes ago gathered on her lashes. Her sister looked horrid. Ashen complexion, dull-eyed and blood-spattered. But she was conscious and coherent. And alive.

"You're going to be fine, Stacy. I need to call 9-1-1. I don't have a phone on me. I dropped it when he came at us."

Stacy grimaced. "Yeah. I think mine is still in the car."

"I think the only reason either of us is alive is because he didn't want our blood in his precious ride."

"His avarice served a good purpose, for once."

"Well, I think maybe God was on our side here. He worked all things out for good, just like it said in Genesis."

Her sister scoffed weakly. Stacy's lack of faith hurt Fran's heart, but she didn't preach, knowing it would only stiffen her sister's resistance to hearing about the love of God. After what she'd been through, Fran wasn't about to add to her distress.

Fran scrambled over to her evil brother-in-law. He remained out cold. Reaching into his coat pocket, Fran grabbed his cell phone, nearly retching at having to touch him. Forcing her thoughts away, she dialed 9-1-1.

Leslie's familiar, perky voice answered the call.

"Leslie, it's Francesca Brown. I'm at my house, in my husband's work shed. My sister's been shot. I have the shooter tied up with zip ties. Not sure how long they'll hold once he wakes up.

"Okay. Stay on the line, Fran. Is your sister conscious?"

Leslie's voice was perfectly professional, yet Fran detected the concern layered in the well-known tone.

"Conscious, yes, but she's bleeding from her shoulder. She's pale and in pain. I'm going to cover her up and raise her legs. But I'm concerned that she might go into shock."

Or bleed out. But she didn't want to say that.

"Help is on the way. ETA is seven minutes."

Seven long minutes. But she couldn't do anything about that.

Fran focused on what she could do. Gathering up the thick Carhartt coat Sean had kept on a hook in the corner, she brought it to her sister and covered her up. Then she took the toolbox he kept stocked for emergencies and wedged it under her sister's feet, raising them six inches off the floor.

"Okay, Stacy. I'm going to check your wound."

Her sister didn't complain. Her lack of response concerned Fran, but she kept her fear off her face, putting on her professional persona to get through these next few minutes.

The bleeding had slowed. She replaced Stacy's weak grip with her own and applied pressure. Stacy whined wordlessly.

"Sorry. I have to put pressure on it." How much longer? "Hold on, sis. You're going to make it. Just a few more minutes."

"If I don't… Lucy…"

"No. You don't need to worry about your daughter. You'll see her again. Very soon. Just hang on. Don't give up."

"If I don't…" Stacy persisted, "you need to know. Chad hired someone to kill you. I heard them arguing."

Fran's heart lodged in her throat. Her sister was more than a victim. She was a material witness to something major. "Could you recognize him?"

"No, but I heard his voice. It was distinctive. I'd remember it."

And she would.

"There's someone in jail now for accepting a contract to kill me. Once you listen to his voice, you'll know if he's the one."

Chad would know that his wife had a condition called hyperthymesia, which was a fancy way of saying that her memory in regard to her own life was nearly perfect. She could recall what she'd talked about on specific dates, and what someone had said to her at a particular time and date. Almost like she was looking back in a book. It also meant she'd be able to look back in her memory to a specific date and recall a conversation. And a voice.

That would have been a reason to kill his own wife.

The seconds dragged by. When the man across the room began to curse and struggle against his bindings, sweat broke out on Fran's upper lip. He was going to get loose. She didn't know what to do. Should she knock him out? It seemed rather coldhearted, but he'd not hesitate to kill them the second he was free.

Sirens wailed in the distance. One zoomed closer, coming to a halt outside. A second siren raised, followed by a third. Two doors slammed. Quiet voices murmured words she couldn't decipher. A few seconds later, a voice called out to her.

"Fran? It's Trey. Are you safe?"

The paramedics had arrived.

"It's safe. Come on in."

The door opened and two paramedics entered the room, pausing long enough to survey the scene for any dangers. Satisfied, they proceeded to where Fran kept vigil over her sister.

She allowed them to take over, scooting back out of their way. Now that the paramedics were present, she ran to the opposite wall and grabbed a hammer. Returning to stand near Stacy's feet, she braced her legs and held the hammer in a double-fisted grip. If Chad so much as sneezed wrong, she'd act. But she wouldn't attack him without cause.

"She's lost a lot of blood," Trey informed Fran. "But her vitals are strong."

The police arrived, coming in hot, sirens blaring and lights flashing through the dusty window. Kathy and Steve charged into the shed, followed closely by Tanner.

The moment his glance fused with hers, Fran relaxed. Stacy would recover. Kathy and Steve had Chad on his feet and were leading him from the shed, reciting his rights as they frog-marched him outside. She was alive and the man who'd wanted her dead was in custody.

And Tanner was there. All was well.

Francesca was safe.

Tanner sucked in a deep breath and released it slowly. He rolled his shoulders once to work out the tension locked in his muscles then strolled over to stand next to her. The paramedics were in the process of loading Fran's sister Stacy onto a stretcher. When he'd figured out who the killer was and then heard Chad Reynolds had been spotted in the area, he'd nearly let his emotions take over and thrown protocol out the window.

"Are you hurt?" He kept his face turned toward the paramedics and their patient. If he looked at Francesca now, she might pick up on how affected he was. He wasn't ready for that. While his feelings ran deep, and he suspected she'd developed some for him, they still had a case to close before their personal issues could take center stage.

Still, the urge to take her in his arms and kiss her for the next hour hammered in his soul.

"I'm not hurt." Something in her voice seemed off. Finally, he turned to look at her. And the desire to take her into his arms intensified. But this time, his desire was to comfort her, to remove the lost expression from her lovely face.

"Tell me."

She shook her head, her dark lashes momentarily hiding her amazing amber eyes. He reached out and gently squeezed the fingers of her right hand. She lifted her chin and the agony on her face hit him like a physical blow.

"I almost lost her, Tanner. My sister has lived with that monster for years. She knew he was capable of heinous things, yet she stayed to protect Lucy. And, to some extent, she stayed to protect me. I failed the three people I loved most in this life. I failed to see my husband was stuck in this mess. Even when we started to learn of it, I'd never guessed how helpless he was. And how could I not see that my sister's withdrawal was a type of abuse? I've worked with victims before. How could I miss it in my own family?"

Her fingers spasmed around his until her grasp became painful. He didn't react. If it would help her come to grips with what she'd learned, she could squeeze his hands until they turned blue. She wasn't really looking at him anymore. Her attention had retreated inward.

"Sometimes we miss things when we're too emotionally close." He kept his voice professional. She needed to hear him. "Francesca, look at me."

He waited until she met his gaze again. "You cannot take ownership of his crimes. Chad is the only one responsible for his bad decisions."

She ducked her head, pressing her forehead against his

shoulder. His heart melted. Poor Francesca. It was a hard thing, dealing with such guilt and remorse.

Now was definitely not the time to express deeper feelings. She needed to come to terms with what she'd learned about her past before she could move forward.

After a moment, she stirred. "There's another thing. Something Stacy heard."

"Tell me in the car on the way to the hospital."

She blinked. "I didn't hear another vehicle drive up. I guess I assumed you came with Steve or Kathy."

He shook his head and caught her hand in his to walk to the SUV. Instantly, he realized what he'd done. He should drop her hand, but she was holding on tight. He let it go and allowed himself to revel in the closeness that sprang up between them.

At the SUV, he opened the door for her, still scanning the environment for any dangers. Only when she was inside the vehicle and buckled did he close the door and jog around to his own side.

"Okay." He snapped his buckle into place and drove away from her house. "What was it that Stacy heard?"

She repeated the conversation she'd had with her sister. He frowned. "Explain this thing she has. Hyper what?"

"Hyperthymesia. Think of it this way. Most people can tell what they did for part of a special day. Like last Christmas, I stayed home and watched a movie. I can't tell you what movie. Or what I ate. But I know I was alone."

That was horribly sad. Something in him cracked knowing she'd spent that holy day by herself. He didn't allow those thoughts to show. Instead, he worked to keep his expression bland and nodded for her to continue. "Go on. I expect that's not the case for Stacy."

"Nope. She can tell you what she was doing at a specific time. Ask her what was on TV at five thirty-two in the evening and, if she was in the house with it on, she can tell you. And not just for last year. For just about every year she can remember at all, she can tell you those facts. So something with any significance, like her husband plotting murder with a stranger, she'll remember. Every word, and the time it happened. If she ever hears that voice again, she'll know it. No mistake. And Chad knows that."

He frowned. "So once she hears Darren's voice, she'll know for sure that he's the man your husband hired to kill you."

"Exactly."

"Leave it to me. I will make sure she has the chance to hear his voice. And if he isn't the man she heard, I'll make sure she's protected." He reached across and put his hand over hers. "When we get to the hospital, I'm going to leave you with Steve or Kathy while I make some phone calls."

"Thank you, Tanner. Really. You've been… Really good to me."

He had the feeling she was going to say something different. It seemed he wasn't the only one holding back.

He was as good as his word. Once they reached the hospital, he found Kathy and told her what was going on. Then he made calls to his SAC and to the chief.

By the time Stacy was out of surgery, a plan was in place. He found Fran sitting in the waiting room and sat down beside her. "Hey. I have something to tell you. It won't be easy to hear."

She sat up straight, bracing herself. "I'm listening."

"As far as we can tell, you are no longer in danger. The only person out for you was Chad."

"And he's in jail."

He shook his head. "Chad is dead."

"What?"

"He had some poison on him and digested it. No one knew it was there. He definitely won't be coming for you. I'm going to collect your niece and make sure she's taken care of until your sister is recovered. Then we will clear up whether Darren Dutcliff was the man she heard. I'm convinced he was. And then you'll both be free to live your lives."

"I can hardly believe it's over."

"It is. Are you ready to go home? You look done in."

Fran nodded. "I want to check on her before we leave. I don't want to let to let the distance form between us again."

He stood and held his hand out to her. When she grabbed it and rose, they walked to the recovery room. "I'll leave you here with her. A guard will be outside. We'll be off as soon as we can."

Frustration bit at him. There were so many things he wanted to say, but knew now wasn't the time. Tanner had always considered himself a patient man, but as far as Francesca was concerned, his patience had begun to wear thin. If only they had more time. But this situation with her sister proved they needed to act quickly.

He wouldn't be able to live with himself if Stacy or Lucy came to harm because he hadn't acted fast enough on their behalf.

They were out of time.

Fran scanned Tanner's face, arrested by the tortured indecision she saw there. Obviously, he had something on his mind. Was it to do with her, Stacy, or the case? Before she could ask, he lifted a hand and placed it along the curve of her cheek. She wanted nothing more than to lean into it.

Then, just as quickly, he removed his hand, leaving her

feeling cold and bereft. Tanner turned and strode away from her. She knew the next time she saw him, he might tell her he was returning to Cleveland.

Dwelling on it accomplished nothing. She needed to be at her sister's side when Stacy awoke. She would be in pain, confused. And probably very scared.

Determined to present a positive face, Fran went back into the room to wait for her sister to wake up.

It took several hours. She tried to read, but nothing could hold her attention. She tried to pray, but it was difficult to find the words. Taking in a deep breath and letting it out on a sigh, she closed her eyes and concentrated on being in the Lord's presence, letting Him take control. He knew what needed to be done better than she did.

Finally, her sister awoke. She was amazingly coherent, though she was groggy.

"Chad?" was the first word out of her mouth.

"He can't hurt you anymore," Fran told her. How much information could she tell Stacy? She pressed her lips together. If anyone deserved to know the truth, it was her sister. "I'm sorry, Stacy. Chad died a few hours ago. He killed himself by swallowing poison."

If her sister wanted the details, she'd tell her. Right now, she didn't want to traumatize her too much.

Two great tears slid out of Stacy's eyes. She turned her face to the wall. Fran gave her a few moments to grieve in peace. She understood. Chad had made some horrible decisions and had let the evil take over his heart, but he had still been her husband. And the father of her child.

Tanner arrived soon after. Stacy was no longer weeping, but she hadn't spoken again. He entered, holding the hand of a little guest.

"Lucy!" Stacy exclaimed when she saw her daughter.

Their reunion was bittersweet. Lucy had never had a close bond with her father, so she didn't seem to be bothered by his absence. Stacy didn't tell her that he was dead. At eight, Fran wasn't sure Lucy would comprehend the meaning of the word.

"Stacy," Tanner began, "has Fran told you what needs to happen now?"

Stacy shook her head, tightening her arm around her daughter. Tanner took her through the next steps quickly. But with great compassion. Her sister paled when he told her she'd see the man's face who'd been paid to murder her sister.

Fran didn't blame her. Knowing someone had ruthlessly ended multiple lives on the whim of one's own spouse would devastate anyone. Not to mention the shadow it would cast over her life from this day on. How did you become close to someone knowing that they might find out about the evil your husband had done. She reminded herself of Tanner's words. It had been Chad's choice. Still, her heart broke for her baby sister.

"Will he know I'm there?" Stacy asked, her voice trembling.

"Stacy," Tanner said. "He won't know. I'm going to show you some footage we took. If you recognize his voice, that should be enough. You will have to testify at his trial. And since he's a hired killer, I've arranged for you and Lucy to go into protective custody until his trial is over."

She hated the defeated look on her sister's face, but it was for the best. Stacy couldn't remain where she and Lucy were in constant jeopardy. The angst of missing them was preferable to experiencing the agony that something tragic had happened to them.

Her sister nodded and Tanner brought out his phone and

let the video play. Within moments, a deep, raspy voice filled the room, eliciting a gasp from her sister.

"That's him. There's no doubt."

An hour later, Stacy, wheeled out through the emergency exit on a stretcher, was loaded into a waiting ambulance. Tanner took Lucy by the hand and secured her in his SUV. A social worker sat in the back seat. Her presence would allow Tanner to concentrate on the drive and hopefully keep Lucy calm. The child was on medications to regulate her tantrums and mood swings. They couldn't risk a sedative that might conflict with them.

Once he was sure Lucy was settled, he turned to Fran.

She could barely breathe around the lump in her throat.

"You know I have to go."

She nodded. "Yes. I understand."

He hesitated. "This isn't the end. I'll be back. I don't know when, but I will. And I always keep my word."

"I'll be here."

He started to turn toward his vehicle. Suddenly, he spun back around and reached for her. She went willingly into his arms, holding on tight. When he leaned down and kissed her, she eagerly responded, wanting him to understand how keenly she'd await his return.

This time, when he let go and stepped aside, he got into his SUV and didn't glance back.

How long would it be until she saw any of them again?

Fran was getting skilled at waiting. She wasn't happy about it, though. She was ready to live again.

She watched the ambulance carrying her sister depart, followed by the SUV carrying her niece and the man who had taken her heart so easily.

SEVENTEEN

"I got your message, Agent Hall," special agent in charge Mitchell announced from the doorway. "I decided to pay you a visit and see what's up."

Tanner's fingers paused on his keyboard for a moment in surprise. "Ma'am! I never meant for you to drop what you were doing."

"Calm down, Agent Hall. I know that." She strode over and eased herself down into the chair next to his desk. "I was in this area and decided to save time. I've been waiting for you to come and see me for the past two weeks."

He sat back in his chair. "Really? Why? Has my work been that bad?"

He'd been distracted, sure, but he'd done his job. He'd been highly motivated. He needed to tie up all the loose ends before he could put his personal plans into action.

SAC Mitchell cast a level stare at him. "Your work's been exemplary, as usual. I was pleased to hear that Anastasia Reynolds has returned home with her daughter."

"Yes, ma'am. The evidence against Darren Dutcliff was overwhelming. So much so that he took a plea deal to escape the death penalty. He'll be in high security prison for the remainder of his life, no hope for parole."

Satisfaction filled him every time he thought of it. Tanner had nearly picked up the phone to call Francesca the moment he'd heard the news, but had stopped himself before he could hit send.

"I'm glad. But I'm talking about your demeanor."

Tanner blinked. "My demeanor?"

SAC Mitchell huffed as if irritated. He didn't buy it. A small smile lurked around her mouth.

"Are you going to repeat everything I say? It's obvious that you've had something on your mind. It was just a matter of time before you came to see me. Now what can I help you with?"

Tanner shifted his position so he was facing her. "I've gotten myself in a bit of a—well…a personal quandary."

She grimaced. "The worst kind. Let me guess. A woman's involved."

Heat suffused his neck and face. "Um. Yes, ma'am."

His superior sighed. "Don't tell me I'm going to lose you too. Your former partner had the same look on his face when he told me he talked to me after reuniting with his ex-fiancée."

Tanner had to laugh at that. Jack had been a bit of a mess after losing his heart to Nicole for the second time. However, while Jack's job had been an issue for them, it wasn't for Tanner.

"I'm in love with Francesca Brown." The words shot out, shocking him. He hadn't intended to blurt his feelings so boldly. This wasn't the conversation he'd planned to have with his superior. Thankfully, no one else was in earshot.

Heaving a heavy sigh, she narrowed her eyes and glared. "Not what I wanted to hear, Tanner. She lives in Sutter Springs, doesn't she?"

Easing a finger along the inside of his collar to relieve the sudden tight feeling, he nodded. "Yeah. And I'm not even sure how she feels about me. I mean, we spent more time trying to stay alive than anything else. Plus, you know, there's the whole issue of Sean."

"The elephant in the room. She didn't know what he'd gotten himself into."

That was an understatement.

"True. She didn't. But still, she might be a little gun-shy of getting involved again. But I need to know."

"And if she isn't gun-shy? If she loves you too? What then?" SAC Mitchell had never been one to beat around the bush.

He swallowed. This was the hard part of the conversation.

"If I'm that fortunate, then I would hope I could transfer to Columbus. That way I'd be close to her."

She crossed her long legs and rested her clasped hands on her knee. "What about asking her to move here? We've got plenty of precincts that would love to contract with an artist of her skill and reputation."

He'd thought about that. "I'm sure there are. But, honestly, when I started thinking of marriage and, hopefully, one day kids of my own, I realized that Sutter Springs felt like home more than Cleveland ever did."

She shook her head. "Well, as much as I hate the thought of losing you, I hope it all works out for you. You deserve to be happy."

"Thanks. It means a lot. I'll keep you in the loop." He hesitated. "I plan on heading to Sutter Springs first thing tomorrow morning."

She nodded and stood. "It's your day off. You can spend it however you choose."

He watched his SAC stride to the door. She half turned and glanced over at him. "If you do end up leaving us, I hope you know you're welcome to come back."

She departed.

Had he done the right thing? He scoffed at himself. Who was he fooling? He'd be no good to anyone until he had an answer. Even if it was no, he'd be able come back, lick his wounds, and then try to carry on business as usual. Although, the thought of trying to continue with the status quo with zero hope made his soul shrivel up inside him.

Did it matter if his boss knew he was thinking of transferring? He wasn't committed to anything yet. If all went his way, though, he would be, very soon.

Restlessness crawled up his legs. He couldn't sit still. Shoving away from his desk, he prowled around the perimeter of the room, stopping to grab a fresh soda from the refrigerator. He opened the bottle and took three healthy swigs before closing it and resuming his pacing. He needed to focus on clearing the paperwork off his desktop. Once he'd filed all the reports, he'd be good to go. With a renewed sense of determination, he resettled in his somewhat battered chair, his fingers working overtime to get the work completed.

As soon as his shift ended, he was out the door and into his vehicle, headed to his apartment to pack for the next two days. He hoped he'd be there that long. In his opinion, if he returned early, he'd have failed, and an empty future would yawn open before him.

He made himself a cheeseburger for dinner and decided to eat in front of the television and watch the news while he ate. By the third story, though, he couldn't take any more. It was all doom and gloom. He might as well turn in and catch up on his sleep before making the drive to Sutter Springs in the morning. It was only two and a half hours away, so he didn't bother to set an alarm. He'd leave when he could.

Two hours later, Tanner groaned and flipped to his other

side. The one night he had time to indulge in extra sleep and he couldn't shut his mind off enough to snooze. Figured. Stubbornly, he stayed in bed, finally drifting off after one in the morning.

The sun was high in the sky when he opened his eyes. Eight thirty. He couldn't remember the last time he'd slept in past seven. Throwing his legs over the side of his bed, he reached for his phone. No messages. He paused. He didn't even know for sure where Francesca was working today. What if he got there and she was in another precinct? He didn't want her to know he was coming.

He thought for a moment then tapped out a text.

Hey. Thinking of you today. Are you working?

He sent the text then waited. Hopefully, she'd read it and answer soon, otherwise—

His phone dinged.

Yep. Thinking of you too. I'm in Sutter Springs this morning.

He glanced at the clock. Francesca hadn't mentioned her afternoon schedule, and he didn't want to tell her he was on his way. If he rushed, he could surprise her and take her to lunch. Some place quiet, where they could talk. He frowned, not liking the idea of expressing his emotions in a public venue. Maybe they could get their lunch to go and eat outside somewhere.

He'd spent enough time lollygagging. Time to put his plan into action.

And hope he didn't make a fool of himself along the way.

It was nearly eleven twenty by the time he got out of his SUV in the Sutter Springs Police Department parking lot.

Praying he hadn't missed her; he speed-walked into the building and checked in. Rounding a corner, he nearly ran Chief Spencer over.

"Whoa! Good morning, Agent Hall. Were we expecting you?"

"Sorry, sir. No, sir. Francesca said she was working here this morning. I wanted to see if she was free for lunch."

"Long drive for a lunch." Chief Spencer smirked. That was the expression of a man well aware of what was happening and wouldn't be deceived by his casual manner. Tanner's ears heated. "She's in the back conference room. I think she's nearly done here. So, whenever she's ready, you all can get out of here."

"Thank you."

"You're welcome, son." The chief continued walking. Tanner could have sworn he heard the man mutter, "About time."

Tanner coughed a chuckle under his breath, unable to keep the sudden amusement at bay. The chief was absolutely correct. It was about time.

He just prayed it would work out in his favor.

Following the hall into the depths of the station, he greeted the officers he passed on the way. Kathy saw him and grinned, wagging her eyebrows. "She's back there, cowboy."

Did everyone know how he felt?

Gritting his teeth slightly, he quickened his steps, anxious for this trial to end. When the conference room loomed in front of him, he slowed his pace again. Approaching the room, he stood in the open doorway for a moment. There she was. Francesca worked behind a laptop, her mouth pursed in concentration. Her sketchpad rested on the table next to her, a sharpened pencil on top of it. From where he stood, he could barely make out the face of the woman she'd completed. Briefly, he wondered what the case was then let it go. He observed her for a moment, his heart swelling, the exhilaration of being near her almost overwhelming his senses.

She sat up and jabbed at a key defiantly. The document disappeared. "There. Done."

He straightened. For better or for worse, he had to discover his fate.

"Tanner!" Fran shoved her chair back so violently her sketchpad and pencil flew across the conference room table and slid into the trash can on the other side. She leaped up then stopped. The urge to throw herself into his arms was strong. Except, she didn't know if he wanted her, if he loved her the way she loved him.

Without a word, Tanner opened his arms. That was all she needed. She hurled herself into his embrace, nearly sobbing in joy when those familiar arms closed around her and held her close.

He'd been gone for three very long, arduous weeks. Fran had buried herself in her work to keep from dwelling on Tanner. She'd been so sure he'd call as soon as Stacy had contacted her. Her sister and her niece were returning to live with her parents.

"I will never set foot in the town where I lived with that monster. We need a fresh start," Stacy had told her.

Joy filled Fran's heart. Her sister's call made it clear that renewing a relationship with her sister was part of her new life.

Her one sorrow was that Tanner didn't call. Had he decided not to pursue a relationship with Fran?

Now he was there. She inhaled deeply, taking in the

scent of his subtle aftershave. A scent she'd forever equate with Tanner.

"Chief Spencer knows I'm here. I was hoping you could manage a lunch break soon but didn't want to make any assumptions."

She nodded. "I've finished the work I had here. I was getting ready to clean up and go, anyway. Let me grab my stuff. I'll let him know I'm done then we can leave."

"Sounds like a plan."

Reluctantly, she stepped out of his arms. Holding his gaze, she reached back and grabbed her purse. Rounding the table, she retrieved her sketchpad and pencil from the trash bin. Fortunately, it had been changed and relined, so they were still pristine.

Instead of returning to his arms, she led the way to the chief's office and knocked on the door. When Mike Spencer invited her in, she stepped into the room and approached the desk. Mike smiled and waited for her to speak.

"I'm done with the composites for the Lawson case." She passed the drawing to him. "I'm booked for the next three days, then I'm at home on call this weekend. I can be back on Monday if you need me."

"Good to know. If we need you, we'll let you know ASAP so you can work it into your schedule."

"Perfect."

The chief angled his head to look around her at the FBI special agent lounging his lanky frame against the door. "Agent Hall, always nice to see you."

"Same goes, Chief."

Fran plopped her sketchpad, now minus the sketches she'd just completed, into her bag and zipped it shut. Nodding at Chief Spencer, she spun and strode briskly out of the office and down the hall, her two-inch heels clicking against the hard floor.

She still only came up to Tanner's nose. She paused at the main entrance, her hand on the release bar. Glancing back at the man who'd become so dear to her in such a short time, she quirked an eyebrow.

"So, where should we go?" She wasn't leaving the air-conditioning until she had a destination. It was nearly the end of September, but the temperature had peaked at ninety-one degrees. And that didn't take into account the humidity.

"Let's go somewhere we can eat and talk privately." Tanner responded.

"My house," she declared. "I have some leftover chicken parmigiana and stuff to make a salad. We'll eat there."

When he agreed, she left him to get into her own vehicle, knowing he'd follow her there. It gave her a few minutes to compose herself before she had to sit across from him. Her heart raced inside her chest, sending blood singing through her veins. The euphoria of being in his presence again overwhelmed her.

It hadn't been that way with Sean. She'd loved her husband, but it had been more of a comfortable love that had grown out of similar ambitions and friendship. He was her first love.

Sometimes she wondered if she would have married him if she hadn't been so eager to escape her parents.

Shaking her head, she let it rest. Whatever she and Sean had shared was over. He'd been a good man, and she'd loved him, but it was time to move on.

Once at the house, she walked up the steps and onto the wraparound porch. Since the events of the past month, Fran had evaluated how she felt about remaining in the house where she and Sean had made their home. But Sean had only actually lived in the house for under a year before his death. Whatever impact he'd had on the place was minimal.

All the love and effort poured into it had belonged to Fran.

What would Tanner think of it as a home?

Stop. She was getting ahead of herself. She didn't know how he felt or what he wanted. He cared for her. That was clear. But he had yet to declare himself.

He parked his new SUV behind her car and joined her on the porch. Without a word, she pivoted away from him and unlocked the front door.

"I'm thinking of getting a puppy," she said out of nowhere.

"A puppy would be a great idea," he affirmed.

Laughing nervously, she let the door swing open and sighed in relief as a wave of cool air hit her face. "Let me get lunch ready, then we can talk. It should only take about five or six minutes since it's already prepared."

"Why don't I do the salad?"

She waved him ahead of her. Within a few moments, they were seated at the table. When he said grace, she had a mental image of what mealtimes as a couple would look like, if that's what he wanted.

He took a bite and chewed, humming appreciatively. "Delicious. What was the occasion? I'm guessing you don't make such deluxe meals when it's only you?"

"That's the truth." She took a sip of water. "After you left with Stacy, my parents paid me a visit."

"Unexpected."

"Yes. Apparently, they felt bad about everything that had happened. When Stacy's husband tried to kill both of us, they realized that the attributes they admired weren't that important."

To her astonishment, she'd received a phone call from her parents a week ago and spoken with both her mother and father at length. The conversation had been awkward and stilted, but it had been a beginning.

Both of her parents had regretted cutting her from their lives. And then Stacy had left to enter the Witness Protection Program. They'd had to face the fact that their own hubris had separated them from both of their children and left them alone. When Stacy returned, they resolved to repair their relationship with both daughters.

She explained their about-face, and her complicated feelings, while he listened.

"How are you feeling now?"

"Mostly, I've forgiven them. But it's hard not to feel a little bitter. After all, the son-in-law they praised turned out to be a cold-blooded murderer. I'm taking it day by day. However, despite all the hurt they've caused me, I do want them all in my life."

He nodded, his expression somber. "Yeah, I get that."

He pushed his chair back and stood. Leaning over, he gathered her plate and silverware, neatly stacked it on top of his own, then carried both to the sink. She watched him rinse and place each dish carefully in the dishwasher without a word. He had that serious little frown he got when he was pondering his next words. She gave him space, knowing he'd voice his thoughts when he'd worked what he wanted to say through in his mind. It amazed her that she had ever doubted his trustworthiness. She knew him so well now.

Finally, he turned and leaned against the counter, his

arms folded loosely across his chest. Behind his wire-framed glasses, his blue eyes glinted, deep and mysterious.

But she knew him. His entire posture bespoke his calm assurance. It was a lie. He was as nervous as a child facing his first day of kindergarten.

How she loved this man!

"The case we were on together is done. You're out of danger, and there's no need for us to work together any longer."

Her stomach dropped. Her mouth dried so fast, she felt like her tongue was glued to the roof of it. Was this his way of saying goodbye? She tried to speak but didn't have the words.

"So," he continued, his gaze pinning her in her chair, "where does that leave us?"

"What do you mean?" She needed some clarity before she could answer.

He pushed himself away from the sink and stalked to where she sat. She rose on unsteady legs.

"I mean, Francesca Brown, I don't want this to be the end. I've fallen in love with you, even though I told myself I shouldn't have feelings for my late friend's wife. But I do. And I don't see that going away. So, I'm asking you, do I have a chance? Because the only way I'm leaving you alone is if you tell me there's no hope."

She felt like she'd received a punch in the gut. She couldn't draw a breath. When his face lost some color, she pushed through the deluge of emotions bouncing inside her and moved close enough his breath ruffled the hair on the top of her head.

"I won't tell you to go." Her words were nearly inaudible over the clash of her heartbeat in her ears. "I've fallen in love with you too."

He huffed a short laugh that ended on a sigh. She was never sure who moved, or maybe they both did, but suddenly they were in each other's arms, her head on his shoulder, holding on tight.

"I asked my SAC if I could transfer to Columbus," he whispered. "She said it would take a few months, but it was definitely doable."

"You'd be so close."

"Exactly." He pulled away so he could look into her eyes. "I'd be close enough to see you almost every day, and eventually, close enough so if we wanted to get a new place or live here, it wouldn't matter."

She arched her eyebrows.

He shook his head. "I'm not proposing. Not yet. I figure we need to have at least one date where no one is trying to kill us before that happens."

"Eventually," she said. She knew what her heart had decided. Waiting another couple of years wouldn't change that. She'd made too many decisions trying to escape the life she hadn't wanted. It was time she took charge and chose the one she did want.

Tanner grinned. "Eventually." He lowered his head.

A tingle of anticipation zipped up her spine. Closing her eyes, she leaned closer and raised herself on her toes.

Her lips met his in a sweet kiss of promise and hope.

EPILOGUE

"Kathy, have you seen my grandmother's handkerchief?" Fran slid her right foot into the ridiculously high white-satin stiletto heel Joss and Nicole had talked her into. Truthfully, once she'd seen the rhinestones glittering along the straps and on the toes, she'd needed no coercing. They were meant for her to wear on her wedding day.

"Here." Kathy handed her the delicate square edged with lace and her grandmother's embroidery. "You left it beside your makeup bag."

"Thanks." Gently, she wound the prized garment around the base of her bouquet, gently pinning it in place. Part of the woman who'd meant so much to her growing up would be at the wedding. "I think we're ready."

Smoothing her hands over the beaded lace of her wedding dress, she glanced in the mirror one last time. She'd fallen in love with the dress the moment she'd seen it. It was slightly off the shoulder and beaded lace decorated the otherwise long sheer sleeves that fell to her wrists. The torso of the dress was lace sprinkled with beads that subtly sparkled as the light caught them. The tulle skirt flared out mermaid style. She felt like a princess on her way to the ball. There was no train. Walking in stilettos would be enough of a challenge. She didn't need the risk of tripping over her own dress and possibly ripping it.

Kathy stepped up to tweak a pin holding her veil in place before letting the filmy fabric flutter over her shoulders and come to rest around her hips. Staring at herself in the full-length mirror, Fran sighed. She nearly pinched herself to make sure she was awake. In a short time, she'd begin her happily-ever-after with her very own Prince Charming.

She grinned at the thought. Tanner would hate hearing himself described that way. But he was her imperfect perfect match. He'd gone through with his plans and had transferred. They'd dated for two months before he'd proposed.

She would have said yes well before that but hadn't said anything, knowing he would ask when he was ready. They'd talked about moving into a new house, but in the end had settled on spending the money on renovating and redecorating the house Francesca lived in. At least for now. They'd worked together the last few months to put his stamp on it so when he moved in after the wedding, it would truly feel like their house.

She didn't care where they lived as long as they were together.

"Don't you dare cry and make your mascara run," Nicole ordered.

She laughed shakily and dabbed her lower lashes. "As if I would!"

Someone knocked on the door. Kathy and Nicole exchanged glances.

"Time for us to go," Kathy stated. Joss stood and followed them out.

After they had left, Fran swiveled away from the mirror and focused her attention on the door, clasping her hands tightly in front of her as her mother entered the room. Fran's palms grew sweaty, but she dared not wipe them on her wedding gown. Looking around, she snatched a makeup blotting cloth off the counter and dried her damp hands with it.

"Mother," she greeted her parent. Their relationship was still strained, even though they'd reconnected eight months ago. She'd visited them a couple of times, but being inside the walls where she'd grown up had nearly given her hives. It would take a long time before the wounds left by their hurtful words and attitude would heal.

To her relief, they weren't pushing for more than she was able to give. She now talked with them every week on the phone. It was a beginning.

They had met Tanner last night at the rehearsal dinner. Fran hadn't asked their opinion of him. To her, their approval no longer mattered. They had cast her off, and although she was open to having them back in her life, she would be cautious. This time, they'd have to earn their way into her trust. Tanner had agreed with her.

"Your father is waiting downstairs," her mother began. "I wanted to give you something before you left for the church."

Fran waited, curious, while her mother opened her silk handbag and withdrew a small pouch.

The older woman's heels tapped on the floor when she crossed the room to her daughter. Her silver shoes sparkled when the sunlight coming through the window hit them. If Fran had gotten anything from her mother, it was her taste in footwear.

"What's that?"

"This is something that should have been given to you before your first wedding." She motioned for Fran to hold out her hand, then tipped the pouch over and poured the contents into her daughter's waiting palm.

Fran sucked in a painful breath, willing herself not to cry. Her grandmother's diamond-and-pearl necklace. "I remember this. Nana wore it every day."

"Yes, she did. Francesca, I'm heartily ashamed of myself. This necklace was left to you in my mother's will. Yet when you got engaged to Sean, I kept it and gave it to Anastasia for her to wear on her wedding. I'd forgotten about it until Anastasia handed it to me the other day, telling me she knew who it really belonged to. I'd like you to have it, though it's your choice if you wear it today or not."

Her hands trembled too much to fasten the clasp. "Help me?"

She turned so her mother could do it. This was the most precious gift her mother could have given her. It was more than a necklace. The gesture spoke of regret and acceptance. It gave Fran hope that a full reconciliation could be possible at some point.

As she turned around, her mother settled her hands on Fran's shoulders. "You're beautiful, Fran. I wish you every happiness."

When her mother leaned over, Fran met her halfway so she could deliver a cool kiss to her daughter's cheek.

"Thanks, Mom."

Her mother smiled. "Your father and I will see you at the church."

Fran nodded. Her father wasn't walking her down the aisle. He'd do it if she asked, she knew, but she hadn't felt ready to make that statement. Instead, she'd asked Chief Spencer. He'd been the closest thing she'd had to a father figure in her life in years.

"Are you sure you don't want your dad to do this?" Chief Spencer asked while they were lining up. She'd opened up to him about the state of her relationship with her folks. "I would completely understand."

"I'm sure."

And she was.

Her wedding was just the way she wanted it. She and Stacy had talked. Although they'd once dreamed of being in each other's weddings, Stacy felt like she didn't want to be in the limelight in any way. She'd informed Fran that she wanted to remain next to Lucy and watch. Fran had understood. And truthfully, she'd been relieved. Although they were closer, her friends were a bigger part of her life now.

The organist changed songs. Joss tossed her a smile and then began to make her way down the aisle with that unique step-pause-step used by bridesmaids and brides.

Nicole was next.

Kathy gave her one last hug then made her way down the aisle.

"It's our song, kid," the chief said, holding out his arm.

She grinned. It was time to get married to her man.

The organ blasted the first notes of the "Wedding March."

Tanner's heart stalled then began to gallop in his chest. He faced the back, barely noticing his groomsmen and the bridesmaids. His entire focus rested firmly on the gorgeous vision in white making her way toward him on the chief's arm.

How had he become so blessed? He blinked the emotion away and she was suddenly there at his side.

For the remainder of the ceremony, her amber gaze staring lovingly into his eyes and her warm, generous smile were the only things he saw. He somehow managed to repeat his vows when instructed. When he slipped the ring onto her finger, he sighed, feeling as if his soul was finally settling into place. He'd been angry when Amber had rejected him. Now he was grateful. All the pain and loneliness was behind him.

Fran had been worth the wait.

His sight blurred. Humbled, he blinked the moisture from his eyes and focused on his gorgeous bride. She smiled just for him, warming him from the inside out. At thirty-nine years old, he'd assumed he'd remain single and alone for the rest of his life.

"I pronounce you husband and wife."

Tanner leaned in and kissed her a second before the reverend said he could. The laughter of the congregation rose and washed over him. At that moment, nothing existed for him but his bride. His wife.

Breaking apart, they grinned at each other. With her hand on his elbow, they proceeded down the aisle toward the back of the church. Tanner's brothers gave him a thumbs-up. His mother mopped the tears off her face while his father rubber her back.

The photographer caught them and drew them aside to begin snapping shots immediately. For the first time since the explosion, Tanner didn't worry about the scars on his neck showing up in pictures. Fran had seen them and hadn't been disgusted. As far as he was concerned, no one else mattered.

"Congrats, Tanner. You look happy."

Tanner turned to his best man and former partner, Jack Quinn. "Thanks, man. I'm sure I will be. Although, I hope I don't walk around with a foolish grin like you. People won't take me seriously."

Jack scoffed. "Too late. You had a goofy smile before you got involved with Fran. Now it's worse."

"Stop," Francesca scolded him. "I like his goofy smile."

Nicole slid her arm through her husband's. "These men of ours are quite the characters."

Both men rolled their eyes.

"Hey," Nicole said in a stage whisper. "Now that we're both married, we need to find someone for Kathy."

Two feet away, Kathy shuddered. "Don't you dare. I like my life just fine."

Francesca raised one eyebrow and glanced at family and friends milling around them. "You know, Tanner has brothers. They're single. I can introduce you."

Kathy made a face before the photographer put an end to their joking.

Forty-five minutes later, they were in the limousine on their way to the reception. Tanner took advantage of the time alone to kiss the lipstick off Francesca's pretty lips. She didn't seem to mind.

When they arrived at the hall, she took a few seconds to slick the classic berry gloss on her lips. He watched her, smiling. "You know, that wasn't a bad idea you had."

She paused, the lip gloss wand hovering near her lower lip. "Which idea was that?"

"The one about setting up my brother with Kathy. I think she and Logan would make a good team."

She gurgled, half laughing and half scoffing. "I don't know. Kathy seems determined to remain single." She paused, biting her bottom lip. He wiped his mouth, hiding the grin. She'd removed half the color again. "You know, she was engaged once."

He sat straighter. "I didn't know that."

She nodded. "I don't know all the details. She doesn't talk about it. But the engagement was broken due to his, uh, double life."

Oh, no. "He was already married?"

She shrugged, but her eyes told him everything he needed to know.

"Okay, so maybe she and Logan wouldn't make a good match. It was just a thought."

He smiled, then changed the subject. "By the way, your wedding gift will be ready when we return from our honeymoon."

Her eyes flared wide open. "I thought we weren't doing wedding gifts."

He grinned and grabbed his phone from his pocket. Pulling up his photos, he found the picture he wanted. A small brown ball of fluff with a wagging tail stared out at them.

She gasped. "You got me a puppy!"

"Don't cry." He put his phone away. "Your friends would never forgive me if I made you cry today. She's six weeks old. I haven't named her yet. But she's a full-blood yellow Lab. We'll have to train her."

The happiness on her face more than made up for any messes they'd have to clean up later.

Setting the thought aside until later, he assisted Fran from the limousine. Hand in hand, they walked into the lobby of the reception hall. The bridal party waited for them. Logan disappeared to inform the DJ that the bride and groom had arrived. When he returned, they took their places.

Soon, the wedding guests were asked to take their seats and then the bridal party was introduced.

"Bridesmaid Josslyn Beck, escorted by groomsman Zachary Hall."

Joss and Zack left.

"Bridesmaid Nicole Quinn escorted by groomsman Logan Hall."

The guests cheered.

"Maid of Honor Kathy Bartlett escorted by best man Jack Quinn."

They were next.

"Ladies and gentleman, please stand and give a warm welcome for our bride and groom, Francesca and Tanner Hall!"

A wave of whoops and claps nearly tore the roof off when Tanner led Francesca through the throng of guests to their seats at the head table. He held the chair back for her then seated himself at her side. Immediately, someone in the crowd, probably his little sister Vanessa, began clinking a spoon against the side of a water glass. It wasn't long before the crowd celebrating with them joined in. Laughing, Francesca turned toward him. Never one to pass up a golden opportunity, he kissed his new wife in front of their guests, knowing his heart had found its forever home with her.

God was good.

* * * * *

Dear Reader,

I first introduced Francesca Brown and Tanner Hall in *Amish Cradle Conspiracy.* At the time, I had no plans to tell their story. But the more I saw them in that book, the more I knew they'd be perfect together. They are two flawed characters who grow in faith and learn to open their hearts. I hope you enjoyed their story.

I love connecting with readers. I can be reached on Facebook and Instagram, as well as through my website at www.danarlynn.com. Consider signing up for my newsletter to keep up with my writing news.

Blessings,
Dana R. Lynn

HARLEQUIN
Reader Service

Enjoyed your book?

Try the perfect subscription for Romance readers and get more great books like this delivered right to your door.

See why over 10+ million readers have tried Harlequin Reader Service.

Start with a Free Welcome Collection with free books and a gift—valued over $20.

Choose any series in print or ebook. See website for details and order today:

TryReaderService.com/subscriptions